A Very Brave Girl

R.A. Kahn

A Very Brave Girl

FIRST EDITION:
October 2022

Cover Image: Hello_Naomi from www.fiverr.com
Layout, Typesetting and Formatting: Shoshanah Shear

ISBN: 9798373168915

For Further Information:
Shoshanah Shear
shoshanah.s@gmail.com
www.creationsfromjerusalem.com

CONTENTS

CHAPTER 1

How it all began

Miss Marjorie Gorley made her way slowly up the path to her cottage in the grounds of the famous Girls School, of which she just happened to be the head teacher. It had been a very long day for her, and now it was almost dark. She had left her torch in her desk drawer and her house was in complete darkness. Miriam Apple, her housekeeper, who was getting on in years, must have left early again, she thought. Well, no sense in hanging around when the work is done, but she had not remembered to turn on the porch light before leaving. It was cold out and Marjorie could hardly wait make herself a hot drink and to put her feet up once she got inside. Finding her key in her pocket, she let herself in and walked quickly in the direction of the kitchen. Switching on the light, she realized at once that she was not alone. A small girl was sitting at her kitchen table, her head resting on her hands.

"Goodness, child, you startled me! What on earth are you doing here? Don't you know that this house is out of bounds?"

The child lifted her head up slowly. She had fallen asleep. She stared at Miss Gorley.

"But I'm not one of your girls, Miss. The housekeeper let me in. She said her name was Miriam Apple, and that she had to go, because her husband, Mr. Apple, is not well. She showed me the guest cloakroom, and then she said that I was to wait in here and not move. That must have been hours ago, because now I see that it is quite dark."

"Well, who are you, if you are not one of ours, and where do you come from? I really think I ought to call your parents at once," said Miss Gorley, feeling quite perplexed.

"You can't do that," replied the girl. "They don't want me anymore and they have gone away somewhere. I was supposed to live here with my Gran, but she had a fall this morning and had to go to hospital. I didn't know what to do or where to go, when the ambulance driver would not let me go with her in the ambulance. Granny said to run next door, but there was nobody there, so I just got on a bus. When the bus driver said that his bus did not go to the hospital, I decided to get off at the very next stop, which happened to be outside this school. I could see girls walking about everywhere, so I opened the gate, the small one near the bus stop and walked in."

"Didn't anyone see you or try to stop you, seeing as you are not in uniform?"

"No, no one seemed to notice me. They all seemed to be hurrying about and so I just kept walking, until I came to this house. I was afraid at first, but then I got brave again and knocked at the door. A kind old lady opened it after a while and said that I had better come in. She brought me in here, to the kitchen and told me to sit down. Then she said it was time for her to go home but that Miss Gorley would be home shortly and that I had better wait. That must have been a long time ago, as I said. Are you Miss Gorley?"

"I most certainly am, and who are you?"

"I'm Elizabeth Sinclair, but mostly I'm called Liz or Lizzie."

"Well Lizzie, where exactly are your parents? I will have to contact somebody. Do you have any other family in Town?"

"No, no one besides my Gran and she's in hospital now".

"Do you happen to know which one she was

taken to? That would be a start, I think."

"Here, it's written on this piece of paper and there's a telephone number, too. The ambulance driver wrote it down for me." Lizzie handed the note to Miss Gorley.

"Well let's have a nice cup of tea first and then I'll have to make a few calls," said Marjorie Gorley kindly but firmly, indicating to Lizzie that she would have no arguments.

As Marjorie filled the kettle, she watched the small girl, who was still sitting quietly at the table. She felt tired and rather irritated. What could Miriam have been thinking? Why hadn't she called through to the Administration block to report the matter? After all, she had been working at the school for over twenty years. Surely, she must have realized that this was a very odd and possibly dangerous situation. Marjorie would have to talk to her in the morning. In the meantime, what was she supposed to do with this strange young girl? Well, first things first, she thought as she made the tea and arranged a plate of her favourite chocolate biscuits. She watched Lizzie sip her tea and nibble at a biscuit. Then picking up her own cup she said, "I'll be back in a while. You can eat a few more biscuits but you must stay here." And with that she left the room, closing the door behind her. She made her way quickly to her bedroom and closed that door behind her too. She put down her cup and reached for the phone, thinking that she would call the hospital first. She was about to dial the number when she realized that she had forgotten to ask the child for her grandmother's name. "How silly of me," she thought, "I must really be tired!" She hurried back to the kitchen. Lizzie was still sitting quietly at the table, another biscuit in hand.

"Elizabeth," she began "Do you know your grandmother's name and the address where you were staying?"

"Yes, Granny is Mrs. Jane Sinclair. She's my father's mother, and she lives at Number 5 Westcliff Gardens. That is where I was staying too, since my parents went away."

"Thank you," said Miss Gorley. "There's a small cloakroom just next to this kitchen, if you need to go Lizzie, but otherwise, please remain here while I make some calls."

"Yes, Miss Gorley and thank you," replied Lizzie, watching as Miss Gorley hurried back to her bedroom down the passage.

The phone rang for quite a while before it was answered, and Marjorie asked if a Mrs. Jane Sinclair had been admitted to the hospital that day.

"Oh, yes," said the receptionist, "I can see her

name on the list. Brought in by ambulance at 10.07 this morning. She's in Ward 6 now, would you like me to transfer this call for you?"

The call was transferred and after a short wait, Nurse Anderson answered. She said that Mrs. Sinclair was awake and resting and that she could certainly talk to Miss Gorley. The nurse added that Mrs. Sinclair had been most anxious for news of her young granddaughter, whom she supposed was home alone now. The call was transferred once again.

Marjorie Gorley introduced herself and said that her granddaughter had somehow found her way by bus to her school and was now sitting in Miss Gorley's kitchen, eating biscuits with a cup of tea. Then Jane Sinclair began to talk.

"You don't know how worried I've been about her. Once the ambulance arrived, I told her to go to my very good friend and neighbour next door, but perhaps Sheila is away, that's Sheila Berry. I've tried to ring her several times and got no reply. She could have gone shopping or to the library, as she often does. Makes a day of it. I simply cannot understand why Lizzie got on that bus. Perhaps she thought she could make her way to the hospital. She was upset when they wouldn't allow her in the ambulance. She has had a very rough time lately.

You see, my son is in the army, and he was posted away again at very short notice. At the last minute, my daughter in law Andrea, decided to go with him. She's a journalist and thought it would be good for her career. I agreed to take Lizzie in, as we have always been close, but the poor child feels that she has been abandoned – that her parents don't really want her, and she simply won't hear otherwise at the moment. I've explained it all to her and that they simply cannot take children into a war zone. Now of course, she thinks that perhaps they will never come back home again. To make matters worse for her, I had this fall this morning – slipped in the bathroom. So silly, really. I am usually very careful. I might have broken my hip. I've been for X-rays, and I am waiting for the results. They seem to be very busy here because I have heard nothing yet. I really don't know what to do with the child – we have no other family here and Lizzie's home, school and all their friends are hundreds of miles away, in another Town.

"Well," said Miss Gorley, "As it is so late in the day now, she will have to stay with us at the school. You've heard of Oakwood perhaps? Our very kind matron will find a bed for her in the sickbay, the san., as we call it, which is thankfully empty at the moment. We keep a supply of toothbrushes and pyjamas or nightgowns, in case of an emergency, so that won't be a problem. It is too late for her to eat with the boarders, but again, Matron will fix her something to eat, I'm sure. I will call again in the morning to see how you are and when you can expect to go home. Good night, Mrs. Sinclair. Do try to get some sleep and please don't worry. Your granddaughter is in safe hands."

Before Jane Sinclair had a chance to say anything more in reply, Miss Gorley had ended the call.

Miss Gorley had three other calls to make and was anxious to get back to the little girl in her kitchen. She called the Matron first and she arrived at Morningside House about twenty minutes later. She had brought her car over so as to take Elizabeth up to the cottage which housed the San. She knocked on the door and Miss Gorley let her in.

In the kitchen, Lizzie was still sitting at the table. She looked a little frightened now. She had made one visit to the cloakroom, and she was very tired. It had been a long and very strange day for her.

"This is our Matron, Mrs. Collins, Elizabeth. She is going to take you up to the cottage for the night. You can have a bath and something to eat and, in the morning, after I have spoken to your grandmother again, we will be able to plan what to do next. I gather that you haven't yet started in a new school since your parents moved you down here. Is that correct?"

"Yes," said Lizzie timidly. "Granny was going to let me settle down a bit first and she wanted to make enquiries about schools. All this happened so quickly, you see. I still don't see why I couldn't have gone with Mom. With Dad in the army, we have been alone together quite often. She has never left me behind before."

"Don't worry about that now, child," said Matron. "You just come with me, and we will have a good chat about it over supper. My car is outside."

"You're in very good hands, now, Lizzie. Mrs. Collins will take good care of you and at least your grandmother knows where you are. I will see you later tomorrow morning. Good night and thank you Mrs. Collins," said Miss Gorley. They walked to the front door together and Lizzie saw Matron's small car just outside the gate.

"Thank you for the tea and biscuits," she said as she waved goodbye and hurried towards the car. It had been a long and very strange day. Lizzie suddenly felt very tired indeed. She was also on the verge of tears, but she was determined not to cry. What an awful day it had been, for her and for her grandmother. She wished she could phone her own mother, but she knew that was out of the question.

They didn't even know where she was, and until her mother contacted them, they wouldn't even be able to write to her. That's why Lizzie felt so abandoned. At least in her grandmother's house, which she had known all her life, she felt almost at home. She missed her parents, and she missed her friends. This was all so awful, but she would just have to be brave, wouldn't she? Mrs Collins seemed so kind and so did Miss Gorley.

CHAPTER 2

Lizzie's first taste of boarding school life

"You can sleep in here, Elizabeth," said Matron, opening the door to a very pretty room. "The bed is made up and ready for you. I will show you the bathroom and you can have a nice warm bath while I find you a pair of pyjamas and make you something to eat. I am sure you haven't had a proper meal since breakfast, have you? Here's the bathroom," she said, crossing the passage and opening another door. "You can use these clean towels on the rail. Call me if you need anything, oh and the soap is in that little dish on the side, do you see?"

"Thank you," said Lizzie, as she closed the bathroom door. This is all so strange, she thought, this morning I was warm as toast in my room at Granny's and now I am here. What would mummy say, I wonder?

As the bath filled, she undressed and folded her clothes into a neat pile, which she placed on a chair near the bath. Taking the soap, she stepped into the nice warm water.

Later, as she was drying herself, Mrs. Collins knocked on the door. She handed Lizzie a toweling dressing gown with matching slippers and a pair of soft, warm pyjamas.

“Those ought to fit you,” she said. “We keep a supply here for emergencies. When you are dressed, come into the kitchen. I’ve made you some scrambled eggs on toast and a mug of hot cocoa. Nothing too heavy, as you have not eaten properly today.” She closed the bathroom door and Lizzie could hear her footsteps retreating down the passage. This must be a very posh school, she thought, as she quickly dressed and tidied up the bathroom. Later, she would say as much to Mrs. Collins. Taking her clothes back to the room she had been allocated, she placed them at the end of the bed and hurried along the passage to find the kitchen.

After the meal, Lizzie brushed her teeth with the new brush and little tube of toothpaste Mrs. Collins had given her. Then she climbed into bed and Mrs. Collins switched off the light.

"I'll see you in the morning and in the meantime, try not to worry about anything. I live in this house, so I'm here if you need me, you only have to call – goodnight, Lizzie, I hope you sleep well."

Lizzie murmured a drowsy good night and in spite of herself and all her troubles, she fell asleep immediately and slept soundly. The next thing she knew it was morning and Mrs. Collins was calling her name.

After breakfast, Mrs. Collins told Lizzie to wash and dress quickly as Miss Gorley would be coming over to see her shortly.

CHAPTER 3

What Miss Gorley said

"I've just spoken to your grandmother, Elizabeth and to her doctor, who said that the fall did more damage than they thought when she was admitted to the hospital. She is having more X-rays this morning but, in any case, your poor Granny will not be coming out of the hospital for quite a while, dear. It is very fortunate that you found your way here because this is a boarding school, and we just happen to have space in our junior dormitory for you. I have discussed all this with your grandmother and because you have a trust fund started by your parents for you, there is enough money to cover your school and boarding fees and your school uniforms. We have a clothing depot right here in the school grounds, so I am sure that we can find everything you need there. Do you still have the key to your grandmother's house?"

"Yes, it is here in my pocket," replied Lizzie.

"Good, then Mrs. Collins will take you there in her car, so that you can collect whatever else you might need. Of course, all your clothing will have to be marked with your name. Your house matron, Mrs. Jordan, will see to that for you. Later, perhaps even tomorrow, we will give you some tests, to make sure you'll be placed into the correct class. Do you have any questions, dear?"

"So, I'm to stay here, until my Granny is better?"

"Yes, that's the idea. You hadn't been enrolled yet in any other school, so that has worked out well, hasn't it? Your guardian angel must have guided you here! It is quite amazing to think how you just got on that bus and got off outside our very gate!"

"Oh, Miss Gorley, I brought my last school report with me. I was in Grade 4 at my last school. Would you like to see it?"

"That would be useful, Elizabeth. How old are you?"

"I'm nine."

"That's what I thought. Well, we will sort out your classes later. Perhaps this afternoon you can visit your grandmother. I expect you are anxious to see her. But that largely depends on the results of those new X-rays. I will check with the hospital later, for you."

"Thank you, Miss Gorley. You're a very kind lady," said Lizzie, trying hard not to cry. Everything had happened so quickly, and it was all rather bewildering for her.

Marjorie Gorley smiled and hurried out to her car. As usual, she had a very full day ahead of her and there was no time to waste.

Mrs. Collins wasted no time either. As soon as she could, she escorted Lizzie to her car. It was going to be a busy day.

CHAPTER 4

Back to Granny's house

Lizzie knew the address and she also remembered some landmarks. It took Mrs. Collins less than half an hour to find the house.

"I thought it was much further," said Lizzie "I was on that bus for ages! And then I suddenly decided to get off, I don't even know why, and I found myself outside your school."

"It's very fortunate that you did, my dear. I don't like to think what would have happened to you otherwise. You could easily have got lost in this city. It's quite a big one you know, and you are new here." As they were talking, an attractive grey-haired lady rushed up to the car.

"Oh, it's you, Lizzie," she said. "I've been so worried about you and Jane. I was away overnight, baby-sitting my grandchildren for my daughter and son in law and when I returned early this morning, Mr. Oliver came over from across the road and said that he had noticed an ambulance outside this house. Whatever has happened?”

Lizzie, remembering her manners, very politely introduced Mrs. Collins first and then she told Mrs. Berry the whole story.

“Oh, my goodness, poor dear Jane! It would have to happen while I was away and I cannot imagine what would have happened to you if you had stayed on that bus, dear. It just doesn’t bear thinking about, does it, Mrs. Collins? Well, let’s go inside now and collect your things, Lizzie. Come to think of it, while you are doing that, I’ll clear the fridge of all the perishables. We can’t have things going off in it and we have no idea how long your granny will be away. I think I should also pack a bag for her. I am sure she will be wanting her own personal items, like her brush and comb and toothbrush and some of her own underwear and nighties, perhaps. We’ve been close friends for so many years, I know she won’t mind me going into her room whilst she is not there. Goodness knows, I’ve been in there often enough to know my way around. I’ll take the bag to her this very afternoon. You hurry along now Lizzie. You don’t want to keep Mrs. Collins waiting and I have my own key, remember. Your gran has one of mine. Makes life easier when you live alone, to know that someone can help in times of need. Although this time, I was away."

And with that Mrs. Berry hurried into the kitchen to attend to the fridge. Lizzie took Mrs. Collins to her bedroom.

"I have a suitcase under the bed," said Lizzie, thankful that she had left the room tidy. Her grandmother was very strict about tidiness and her bed was always made before breakfast. Mrs. Collins nodded as Lizzie pulled out the suitcase and put it on the bed.

"I see that you have a teddy bear. You can bring it with you if you like. I think that you will probably be in the Bluebell dormitory, Lizzie, and all the girls have at least one soft toy on their beds. By the way the ten and eleven year olds, in the Daffodil dorm, also have soft toys, so either way, you'll not be out of place if you do the same. Now, where are your clothes? Underwear first, I think."

Half an hour later they closed the suitcase and Mrs. Collins took it out to the car. They went back inside again for Lizzie's warm coat and raincoat and to say goodbye to Mrs. Berry. She hugged Lizzie warmly.

"Don't worry about anything at all, dear. I can see that you are in very good hands, and it is about time that you were back in school and making friends of your own age. You have been around us oldies long enough," she added with a laugh, "you certainly could not have picked a better school. I know Oakwood quite well. Only good is ever said of it. I don't know how you did it, but there we have it!"

Mrs. Collins looked pleased. "I am quite sure Elizabeth will settle down quickly and love it as all the girls do. Thank you for those kind words, Mrs. Berry."

"Is there a telephone number I can call, Mrs. Collins? I would like to be able to keep in touch with Lizzie if that is allowed." Mrs. Collins gave her a number and said that if Lizzie was available, she would certainly be called to the telephone. If not, a message would be taken. She said it would be best to call in the evening, after the girls had returned to their dormitories, between seven thirty and eight would be a good time, before "lights out" and bedtime. Then she took Mrs. Berry's own number, just to have on hand.

Lizzie suddenly remembered her school report and ran into the sitting room to fetch it from her grandmother's desk drawer, where it had been put for safe keeping.

Having finally said their goodbyes and started back to school, Lizzie wiped a few tears from her eyes.

"My parents don't even know any of this yet," she said and added "Perhaps it is better this way. They'd only worry and there is nothing they can do about it. What do you think, Mrs. Collins?"

"I think you are being a very brave and sensible girl, Lizzie. We will discuss the matter with your grandmother if we are able to visit her this afternoon. That all depends of course, on the results of her X-rays. Perhaps Miss Gorley will know more by the time we get back."

But Miss Gorley did not have any further news. She had called the hospital and was told that Mrs. Sinclair was still in the X-ray department. Apparently, the hospital was very busy that morning and she had been told to call back at lunch time. She sent Lizzie and Mrs. Collins off to the boarding house, to find Mrs. Jordan, the house matron.

Mrs. Jordan was a warm, motherly lady. She greeted Elizabeth with a hug, took her suitcase from Mrs. Collins, and showed them the way to the junior dormitories.

"You are very lucky that we have one bed free in Bluebell," she said, "Usually we have a full house by this time, but the girl who was to have come to us at the beginning of term, two weeks ago, sadly had a horse-riding accident and will not be able to take up her place for some time, if at all. Here's your bed and you will be sleeping next to sweet little Mary Johnson. She's only eight, but she is quite mature, and I am sure you will get on with her very well. You'll get to know all the other girls soon enough. We have quite a few rules and I am very strict about them, but we will get to all that later," she said, but with a twinkle in her lovely brown eyes. "Let's unpack what we can now, into your top drawer, here, but none of your clothing yet, as I am going to have to put your name on everything first. Will 'E. Sinclair' do? We don't have any other Sinclairs here, so that should be fine. Put your teddy on the bed now if you like. You can see that each child has something soft to cuddle at night, so I'm glad that you've brought him along."

Lizzie settled her precious bear on the pretty blue quilt, where he looked quite at home, resting against the pillow. She noticed that all the quilts were blue but that the curtains were floral, bluebells on a pale green background. There were small green mats beside each bed too, giving the whole room a fresh and welcoming look.

"I think I love it here already," whispered Lizzie and the two matrons smiled.

"Now you'll need your school uniforms, dear," said Mrs. Collins. "Let's get down to the clothing depot. All that will have to be marked, too. Rather a big job for you, Mrs. Jordan," she added.

Mrs. Jordan just smiled. "It will all be done in good time," she said, "Not to worry."

Goodbyes were said and Lizzie and Mrs. Collins were on their way again.

"Let's see if we can get all this over with before lunch. That will give us a full hour. Then I will take you to the junior dining room myself. I eat in there as well, with several of the teachers."

CHAPTER 5

The clothing depot and the junior dining room

Lizzie was amazed to find that the clothing depot was set up just like a real shop. Row upon row of school dresses hung neatly on rails, with more rails containing blazers. There were drawers and shelves full of tracksuits in various colours; school socks; and two shelves of hats, for both summer and winter. In no time at all, the very efficient Mrs. Simpson had Lizzie measured and fitted and her pile of clothing placed on the counter.

"Now," said Mrs. Simpson, "What house are you in, Elizabeth? Each house has its own colour, so I can't get your sports clothes until I know." Mrs. Collins explained that there were three houses, Ash; Birch and Elm, all named for great trees. Ash was red, Birch was blue, and Elm was yellow. "I'll phone admin and ask if you have been placed in one yet," she said.

Lizzie hoped she would be in Birch because blue was her favourite colour. Sure enough, a few minutes later Mrs. Collins announced, "Birch it is, dear! So, your colour is blue."

Mrs. Simpson produced the blue T-shirts and shorts and added them to the pile, together with a swimming costume.

"That ought to do it. I will see that all this gets to Matron for you, so it can all be marked. I suggest that you change into a school dress now, Lizzie. It's almost lunch time and you'll want to fit in in the dining room on your first day, won't you?" Lizzie changed and her own clothes were added to the pile to be sent to matron. She put her grandmother's house key safely into the pocket of her new uniform. Then she and Mrs. Collins hurried down to the junior dining room, which they reached just as the lunch bell rang.

Mrs. Collins explained that the day girls could bring their own packed lunches, if they preferred to. They ate those in a special common room if the weather was too cold or wet to eat at the tables outside, under the beautiful oak trees which surrounded the school grounds.

There were four long tables in the junior dining room, each seating ten boarders. There was also a special table for the teachers and staff and another for any day girls who had chosen to have a cooked lunch, instead of bringing a packed one from home.

"We'll wait and see where there is a space for you, Lizzie. All the girls keep the same places and each of them has a special napkin ring holder, you'll see. I'll have to find one for you. There's a box of spare rings in the kitchen. Girls tend to leave them behind when they move up to the senior dining room, you see, but we'll get you seated first."

Lizzie was pleased to find that her place was to be between the very pretty fair-haired Rosie Bishop and Mary Johnson, who had lovely dark curly hair and who would also be in the bed next to hers in the Bluebell dorm. All the girls stood behind their chairs until the teachers were in their places. A special little prayer was said and then the oldest girls lined up at the kitchen door. They would serve each of the other girls in turn.

As Lizzie was about to sit down, Mrs. Collins announced "Girls, we have a newcomer with us today – Elizabeth Sinclair, known as Lizzie. I hope you will all give her a warm welcome." All the girls clapped, and a few called out, "Welcome to Oakwood, Lizzie!"

Lizzie, who was not expecting this at all, blushed, but managed a muffled "Thank you," all the same.

Soon a plate of food was set in front of her and as she tucked into the delicious stew, she realized that she was indeed very hungry. “My very first boarding school lunch,” she whispered to herself, “and it is so good!”

CHAPTER 6

Tests and a special visit

After the meal, Mrs. Collins introduced Lizzie to Miss Price, who would take her to the library, where she was to complete some tests. Miss Price greeted Lizzie very warmly. She was quite tall and was dressed in a smart pale grey skirt, with matching floral blouse. Her hair was light brown, and she wore it in a neat ponytail. She had grey eyes and a very pretty smile. Lizzie felt at ease with her immediately. Miss Price explained that the other boarders would go to their dormitories for the rest period they had every day after lunch. Mrs. Collins added that when the tests were completed, she would see if it was possible to visit her grandmother. Visiting hours in the afternoons started at three o'clock. It would not matter too much if they arrived a little late, but that they would have to leave at four, like all the other visitors. Miss Price said that would be fine, because Lizzie would only start proper lessons the following day, in any case.

So Lizzie, having thanked Mrs. Collins for perhaps the eighth time that day, followed Miss Price to the Library. To her surprise, this was in a separate building all on its own. It was very spacious. There was a large entrance way with display cabinets down both sides in which Lizzie could see artwork and projects all made by the students, and each one neatly labelled with the student's name, project name and grade. They entered the actual library through double glass doors. Miss Price explained that it was divided into three sections. Through an archway, Lizzie could see the junior library, with masses of books on shelves within easy reach of younger children. At the end of each row of shelves were padded benches and colourful beanbag chairs were scattered all around. Lizzie noticed that several beanbags were already occupied, obviously by young day girls, who were all happily absorbed in their books. The senior section of the library was more than twice the size of the junior one, but here again there were comfortable reading spaces in between the many shelves of books, all of them occupied by girls busily reading. The third section, Miss Price said, was the Teachers' library and was strictly out of bounds to all students. This area was separated from the senior section by 10 large wooden tables and chairs. On some of the tables Lizzie noticed daily newspapers but on two of them were jigsaw puzzles. Miss Price again explained that any girl was welcome to add pieces to a puzzle any time they had a free moment. Three girls were busy trying to do that and were obviously enjoying themselves.

The librarians themselves, of which Lizzie could see two, were seated behind a long wooden counter, at the front and to the left of the entrance. Further along, Lizzie saw a row of computers. Miss Price led Lizzie to a row of cubicles behind the worktables. Each cubicle contained a table and two or three chairs.

"We'll do your tests in here, Lizzie," she said, "Please sit down." She placed the briefcase she was carrying on the table and withdrew a pile of papers, a story book, pencils, and an eraser. Lizzie was excited to see that the book was a copy of "Pippa's Island" by Belinda Murrell, which she had read before and loved.

"Let's start with reading," said Miss Price, placing the book in front of Lizzie. "Can you read a few pages of this for me? Start at the beginning if you like."

Quickly and fluently and with lots of expression, Lizzie read through the first six pages.

"Excellent!" said Miss Price, making a note on her pad. "Now here are several words for you to look at. Take a minute to read through them and then I will ask you to write them down, unseen, as I call them out. After that, we will do some Math. This way I will be able to place you in the right grade. I have read your school report and I gathered that you are a very keen learner, and all your marks were good, but let's make sure. Standards differ sometimes between schools, and we do want you to be happy here at Oakwood."

Lizzie managed all her tasks very well indeed and Miss Price would be able to report very favourably to Miss Gorley. She was further impressed when Lizzie thanked her and said that the tests had been fun!

Mrs. Collins arrived at that moment. "Well, Lizzie," she said. "I've good news and bad news, I'm afraid. Your granny's injuries were far more serious than she had thought at first, and she will have to have a hip replacement operation in a few days' time. So she will be in hospital for a while, and because she lives alone, except for you, of course, the hospital has arranged for her to go from there into a lovely place called a convalescent home. They will care for her there until she is ready to safely return home. So, it is just as well that you found your way here, isn't it! The good news is," continued Mrs. Collins, "that we can visit your granny today. She is resting now because they have given her some medication to make her more comfortable. So, you and I have just time for a nice cup of tea, and then if you tidy yourself, we'll be on our way!"

CHAPTER 7

The hospital visit

Lizzie had never been inside a large hospital before. The bright lights; the strange smells and so many people rushing around everywhere, frightened her a little. Mrs. Collins, sensing this, took Lizzie's hand as they walked up to the information desk. Mrs. Jane Sinclair was now in room 207 on the second floor, in a ward called "Women's Surgical". The lady behind the counter informed them that there was another visitor with her, and Lizzie guessed that it would be Mrs. Berry. She relaxed a little. She was fond of kind Mrs. Berry.

When they knocked on the door of 207, which was open, Lizzie peeped inside and was relieved to see Mrs. Berry sitting on a chair next to her grandmother. Looking up and seeing Lizzie she called for them to come in. She was very pleased to see them too.

Lizzie rushed up to her granny and hugged her tightly. “Oh Gran, I’m so pleased to see you. I’ve had such an adventure, but I want to hear about you first before I tell you about me.”

Her grandmother smiled and stroked her hair. “From what I’ve already heard from Sheila here, you have been a very brave girl indeed,” she said. “What a silly thing to have happened to me and now it seems that I will be out of action for quite a while. I am so relieved that you just happened to find your way to Oakwood, and that they have all been so good to you. You must be Mrs. Collins? I can’t thank you enough for all you have done for my young girl here. She has been through so much herself, in the last few months.”

Mrs. Collins nodded. “It has been a pleasure to help, Mrs. Sinclair. Elizabeth is a very mature girl for her age, and she has been no trouble at all.”

“Of course, I know all about Oakwood and I couldn’t be happier, knowing that Lizzie is there. Her mother will be pleased too. Talking of her, I do suppose that I ought to get a message to her somehow, just to fill her in on all that has happened. However, I can only do that when we have her exact location. We are not allowed to know where my son is at the moment, but Andrea promised to write as soon as she was settled. I suppose she has been moving around quite a bit. I did have two short messages from her when she arrived, but we have not been in contact since."

"I've brought your mail, Jane. Here, perhaps there is a letter amongst all this" said Mrs. Berry, handing her friend a bundle of mail. Jane Sinclair glanced through it all quickly. "Oh! Here you are Lizzie, this one is for you!" she said, handing her granddaughter a strange looking envelope. "It's from your mom!" Lizzie tore it open at once and started reading it aloud.

My dearest Lizzie,

Here I am in a very strange land
where everything is hot and dusty
and where the traffic is crazy,
and the food is awful! At least it
seems that way to me.

I want you to know that you are
always on my mind and in my
heart. I hope you and your
granny are enjoying each other's
company and that you are now in

school and working hard.

Take good care of yourself, darling. You can write to me at the above address.

It will get to me eventually. I am on the move gathering information for my job and I don't always have an internet connection.

I will write to you every week, and to Granny Jane.

With love, hugs, and kisses,

Mummy.

"Well, now we will be able to tell her all that has happened," said Lizzie, when she had finished reading. She folded the letter and put it in the pocket of her new uniform. Then she thought of something.

"I don't have any writing paper with me, though."

"Not to worry, dear," said kind Mrs. Collins, "The school has plenty of paper and envelopes and the post is collected every day by our driver, who takes it all to the main post office. If you write as soon as we get back, your letter will go in tomorrow's mail, isn't that good?"

"Will you write for me, too, Lizzie?" asked her granny, "I'm just a little too tired now to think of such things."

"Of course I will, Gran. I will tell Mom everything and I'll tell her not to worry about us. That's especially important, isn't it? I felt so angry when they both went away and sent me here to you, Gran. But now I have accepted it. I KNOW Mom loves me and that I haven't really been abandoned. Besides, I will have to take care of you now, Gran!" she laughed. Her grandmother smiled and pulled her into a hug. "You are doing a great job of taking care of both of us, darling. Everything is going to be all right, isn't it? You're in very good hands, I can see and so am I. Just give Sheila your mother's address dear, and I am sure that Miss Gorley will want to have it too."

Mrs. Collins nodded in agreement.

All too soon the bell sounded for the end of the visiting hour. Mrs. Berry asked Mrs. Collins if she could call for Lizzie and bring her to visit her grandmother again and that was agreed.

They said their goodbyes and Lizzie promised to phone, if she was allowed to, in a day or two.

"Get better quickly Gran," she said, with a last farewell hug.

The visitors went downstairs together, and Mrs. Berry wrote down Andrea Sinclair's address. She said that she too, would write to her that very evening.

Lizzie was very quiet on the way back to the school. Mrs. Collins took her back to the house where she had spent the night before and gave her paper and a pen to write to her mother. In the end, Lizzie wrote three whole pages, in her best handwriting, telling her mother everything that had happened. Then she put the letter in an envelope and Mrs. Collins addressed it for her.

"We'll go down to the main building now and I'll show you where to post this. There's a special box there, just like a real post box. As I said at the hospital, Mr. Hartford will collect it and all the rest of the mail, in the morning."

After that, Mrs. Collins took Lizzie back to her dormitory, where she could bath and change for supper. To her delight, Mrs. Collins informed her that every night after supper, they had story time, when Matron Jordan would read to them before "lights out" and bedtime.

CHAPTER 8

Lizzie's first night in the dorm and story time

Matron Jordan came into the Bluebell dorm, pulled up a chair from the bed nearest to her and sat down. "Come on girls," she said, "Gather round. Tonight, we are starting a new book and that is very lucky for our new girl here, Lizzie Sinclair. Have you all met her?" Most of the girls said they had, but they all turned and smiled at Lizzie.

The girls quickly settled themselves on the nearby beds and waited eagerly for Matron to begin. She was an excellent reader and read with a great deal of expression, changing her voice for the different characters. She had just finished reading her favourite book from her own childhood to them, "The Secret Garden," by Frances Hodgson Burnett. They had all enjoyed it too. Now Matron held up a more modern book. "Has anyone read this book yet?" she asked. The girls nearest to her read the title "Harry Potter and the Philosopher's Stone", by J.K. Rowling. Three of the girls said yes, they had but they would love to listen to it. Lizzie was delighted. She had heard of the Harry Potter books but hadn't yet managed to get hold of one.

Matron began and they were all whisked away into the enchanted world of magic and mayhem. When story time was over, everyone groaned. None of them could wait for the next evening's reading!

"Off to bed, now all of you, and remember dears, no talking after light's out!"

"Good night, Matron," said all the girls together, as they started to prepare for bed.

By the time Lizzie actually got into bed, she was so exhausted from her busy day, that she fell asleep almost as the lights went out. She had no time to feel homesick or even to give her family a thought. Perhaps that was a good thing. She had certainly been very brave, as she faced so many changes all on her own.

CHAPTER 9

The first day in her new class

Lizzie was woken by someone calling her name.

"Lizzie, Lizzie, wake up it's 7 o'clock and breakfast will be in half an hour!"

For a moment, Lizzie couldn't remember where she was, but as she opened her eyes, everything came flooding back to her. Mary Johnson was standing next to her. "Didn't you hear the wake-up bell? We are supposed to get up when the bell goes, because we have to wash, dress and make our beds before we go down for breakfast. Hurry up now or you'll be late."

Lizzie jumped up. "Oh, Mary, I didn't hear the bell, I was so fast asleep. Thank you for waking me." She hurried to the bathroom and back again to dress and make her bed. She was ready just as the breakfast bell rang.

The girls from Bluebell and Daffodil dorms trouped downstairs together to the dining room.

"We always sit in the same places," said Mary, as they made their way to the table. Lizzie thought that breakfast was grand. They started with delicious porridge, followed by hard boiled eggs and buttered toast and a cup of very welcome hot tea.

"After breakfast we go back upstairs to brush our teeth, wash our hands, and collect anything we might need for the morning. Then there is assembly in the hall and after that we go to our classes," explained Mary. "I don't suppose you know where your classroom is yet but don't worry, your teacher will show you. All the teachers come to assembly."

And that is exactly what happened. Lizzie found that her class teacher was none other than Miss Price, who had been so kind to her the day before and she was pleased. Miss Price was waiting for her at the door of the hall when Lizzie and Mary arrived.

"I'll show you where the rest of your class are sitting," she said, guiding Lizzie past rows of girls, who were sitting quietly. "They are in this row here." Lizzie thanked her and sat down as Miss Price walked to the side of the hall, where the rest of the staff were already seated.

Lizzie enjoyed her first assembly at Oakwood and listened carefully to all the notices as they were read out. Junior choir practice would be in the hall after lunch today, she heard and wondered if she could try out for that. She had been in the choir at her previous school, and she loved singing. She would have to ask Miss Price later, if she got the chance.

Ten minutes later she followed the other girls down several corridors to her new classroom. It had a blue door with Miss Price's name and Grade 4 on it. Inside the room was very bright and cheerful, with posters, a large map of the world and some very attractive artwork, obviously done by the girls themselves. There were the usual rows of single desks and Miss Price was there to show her where to sit. She brought Lizzie a pile of books and a school backpack, which contained pens, pencils, a ruler, and eraser. Wow, thought Lizzie, they really think of everything here! She was most impressed.

"Now everyone," said Miss Price, when all the girls were seated. "As you can see, we have a new girl today. This is Elizabeth Sinclair, who likes to be called Lizzie. She has joined Oakwood as a boarder. We welcome you very warmly, Lizzie." At that, the other girls clapped heartily. Miss Price returned to her table in the front. "Beverley, would you be Lizzie's guide for the day?" she asked.

The girl sitting across the aisle from Lizzie said

"Yes, certainly, Miss Price" and she turned and smiled at Lizzie, who immediately felt that they would be good friends. Beverley had a dimpled smile, sparkling blue eyes and she wore her golden-brown hair in a neat ponytail. She seemed full of confidence, too.

The girls settled down and the lessons began.

At ten thirty, a gong chimed in the distance.

"Break time," announced Beverley. "Leave all your things here and follow me. I'll show you where the boarders have their morning tea and sandwiches. I'm a day girl, so I have my tea with me. I'll stay with you and show you around a bit, after we've eaten."

But it wasn't until Lizzie had been there for two more days, that Lizzie was actually able to follow Beverley around the magnificent school grounds. They had been interrupted on that first day by a senior girl, who told them that she had to take Lizzie up to the office to see Miss Gorley.

CHAPTER 10

What Miss Gorley had to say

The senior girl, who introduced herself as Penny Morrow, took Lizzie right to Miss Gorley's office and knocked on the door.

"Come in," said Miss Gorley.

"Here's Lizzie for you, Miss Gorley," said Penny and to Lizzie she said that she would wait outside to show her back to her classroom later.

Everyone is so kind here, thought Lizzie and in fact after she had said good morning to Miss Gorley, she said as much. Miss Gorley smiled.

"Kindness is one of our most important mottos here, dear," she replied, "I think it is what matters most, don't you?"

Lizzie nodded and suddenly felt her eyes fill with tears. She looked down at the beautiful carpet and blinked hard. Miss Gorley, pretending not to notice

Lizzie's distress, continued.

"I've got news for you about your grandmother. She is in surgery having her hip repaired as we speak, so you will not be able to visit her today, dear. You do understand, don't you? I will be in touch with the hospital this evening and I will let Matron know what I find out. In the meantime, you can get to know your surroundings here. Have you managed to make any friends yet, Lizzie?

"Yes Miss Gorley. Beverley Cornhill, who sits next to me in class and Mary Johnson, whose bed is next to mine in Bluebell. Beverley said that she would show me around when we have time."

"That's good, dear. I am sure you will soon feel quite at home here. The school grounds are extensive, so it is important to know your way around as soon as possible. Penny will take you back to your class now and please try not to worry, your grandmother is in good hands."

Lizzie joined Penny and together they walked back to the classroom where Beverley was waiting for her outside the door.

"We have an art lesson now," she said. "I'll take you to the art room."

Lizzie's heart lifted. She loved art classes and her previous art teacher had told her that she was very good at drawing. She enjoyed painting too and wondered what they would be doing during this lesson. They arrived a little late and found the others already seated on square stools around tables set in a horseshoe arrangement, leaving the centre free for the art teacher to walk round, as she watched the girls work.

Beverley introduced Lizzie to their teacher, Miss Gilbert, who was tall and slim, her long dark hair held back with a beautiful hair clip. She wore a long flowing skirt in shades of light and dark purple and a light mauve blouse to match. Lizzie thought her quite lovely. She was definitely going to enjoy this class! She took her place at the table beside Beverley and their lesson began.

CHAPTER 11

The school tour

After second break the next day, Beverley took Lizzie down a long covered corridor which ended at the steps of a lovely old house.

"This is Maplewood," she said. "It is out of bounds to us juniors, but I wanted to tell you about it. The house once belonged to a lady called Harriet Maple, who became the first matron here. She was also the grandmother of the very first head girl of Oakwood. This is where the prefects have their common room and there are also study rooms for the girls writing their final school exams. Usually, we have to be very quiet and keep away from here. All the rooms along the corridor behind us are senior classrooms. Isn't it a pretty house though, Lizzie? You should see the garden at the back. If we are very quiet, I'll show you. Come on."

They crept around the side of the house and Lizzie couldn't believe her eyes at the beauty they saw. The garden was surrounded by old fruit trees and narrow paths wound between beds of glorious roses. There was a stretch of lawn and against the far wall under the trees, were three benches, each set in a semi-circle of bright flowers.

"Oh, wow, this is so pretty," whispered Lizzie in awe. "Who does all the gardening here, do you know?"

"Yes," whispered Beverley in reply. "Mr. Vincent is in charge, but the seniors are allowed to do weeding and stuff. They are also allowed to pick flowers for their desks in the study rooms. We all get fruit when it's ripe, handed out at lunch times and sometimes even at afternoon tea. There are apples; pears; and right over there are plums."

"How do you know so much?" Lizzie wanted to know.

Beverley laughed. "My eldest sister is a prefect now and she told me. You'll meet her soon – Susan Cornhill. My other sister, Patricia, is in Grade 8, and my mother is an old girl. She was a prefect too, so that's why I know so much!"

"Wow," said Lizzie again. "I'm so glad you're my friend, Bev. I have so much to learn about this school. My other school grounds were much smaller and there were no boarders, but we did have boys!"

"I've got two brothers," added Beverley. "Peter, who is the oldest of all of us and Brian who is the youngest. I'm closest to Patricia, though. We are great friends, and we even share a bedroom, just because we want to. You'll like her, I'm sure. She looks just like me, only taller, because she is older. She's such fun and really good at sport, especially swimming. Oh, I haven't taken you down to the sports fields yet, or the pool. We'll have to do that tomorrow. I have to get my homework ready now, or the bus will leave without me. Did you know that we have our own school buses? I'll have to show them to you too, and the gym. Come on, let's run back to the classroom the back way, because we are not allowed to run in the corridors – for our own safety, we are told. Follow me!" And with that Beverley sprinted off at full speed around the other side of Maplewood House, with Lizzie running behind. She found it hard to keep up with her.

"Gosh, Bev!" panted Lizzie, "you must be an athlete!"

"No, not really, I just need to catch my bus!"

They said goodbye to each other at their classroom door.

Lizzie made her way to the junior common room, which Mary had shown her the day before. Each girl had her own locker, and Lizzie had put her library book in hers. She collected it now and settled down to read. Lizzie loved reading. She had selected a book in the “Pippa’s Island” series. It was an exciting story, and she was still reading happily when she heard the bell ring. Putting the book back in her locker, Lizzie hurried upstairs to bath and change for supper.

CHAPTER 12

A letter for Elizabeth

Three weeks later, Lizzie was standing in the dining room, waiting to be seated, when a prefect came in with a bundle of letters. There was silence as the girls waited anxiously to see if they would be lucky enough to get a letter or a card. Lizzie was daydreaming. She had almost given up hope of hearing from her mother, but suddenly she heard her name being called. She looked up quite startled out of her daydream and hurried to collect her letter. It was only the second one she had received from her mother since she and her father had left.

Mom must have received my letter, Lizzie thought, as she put the letter in her pocket to read later. Lunch was now being served and although Lizzie was hungry, she could hardly wait for the meal to be over, even though someone had whispered that there would be apple crumble and custard for dessert.

Lizzie rushed upstairs as soon as she could and flopped onto her bed. Tearing the envelope open, she smoothed out the pages and began to read.

"My darling girl",

she read, wiping away the tears which threatened to blur her vision.

"I miss you so much! I have just received your letter and was alarmed to read of Granny's fall and all that happened to you afterwards. You are a brave, brave girl, just like your Daddy and I can hardly wait to see you again. I am looking forward to receiving more letters from you soon. I do hope that you have settled into your new school and that Granny is making good progress and will soon be well again.

The news here is bleak, I am working hard under very bad conditions. I can't say more because this is a war zone, as you know. I just hope that you receive this letter and the others I have written to Granny, care of dear Mrs. Berry. I know you will be very good and listen to your teachers, as you always have. In that respect, I am very proud of you, Lizzie.

Have fun with your new friends, darling and I do so hope to hear from you again soon.

With all my love, as always,

Your Mom."

Lizzie read the letter through from beginning to end three times. She was very worried about both her parents, but so glad to have found her lovely school, Oakwood. Everyone was so kind, especially the teachers and dear Miss Gorley. Lizzie doubted if there was a nicer Head teacher anywhere, and as for the Matrons, they were so motherly that no one could possibly be homesick for long under their care.

Putting the letter carefully in her pocket when the bell rang again for classes, Lizzie went off to find her friend Beverley. It would soon be half term and Bev had asked Lizzie to join her for the weekend. Her mother had suggested that she bring a friend home with her. The more the merrier, she had said.

She really loved a full house! Miss Gorley had been pleased with the idea too, when Lizzie went to ask her for permission to go.

"You'll have a great time, Elizabeth," she had said. "I know Beverley's family well. Did she tell you that her mother is an old girl? She was a prefect, if I remember, but that was just before I came here." Miss Gorley smiled.

"Yes, Beverley told me all about her family, Miss Gorley, and thank you, I am really looking forward to meeting them all. But I won't wish away the time because I really love it here."

"I know you do, dear and I am very pleased with the way you have settled down. All your teachers are pleased about it too. Now, about your grandmother. You do know that I have been in touch with the hospital, and they tell me that Mrs. Sinclair is making good progress too. She will be transferred to a convalescent home any day now, where she will be very well looked after. She will also get the further treatment she needs there and daily physiotherapy. She will not be ready to go home for at least another month, so we will make arrangements for you to visit her there, as soon as she has settled in. I've assured your grandmother that she has nothing to worry about as far as you are concerned. So, keep up the good work!"

“Yes Miss Gorley. Thank you.”

“Now off you go and tell Beverley that you have my blessing to go with her at half term.”

Lizzie was so excited that she almost ran back to her classroom to find Beverley. Luckily, she remembered the “no running” rule just in time. She had quite forgotten that Beverley had a music lesson that afternoon.

“Oh, I’ll just have to tell her tomorrow,” said Lizzie, half aloud. She picked up her new library book which she had selected that afternoon, and made her way to the junior common room, where she settled down on a comfortable beanbag to read.

CHAPTER 13

Half term weekend

Beverley was very pleased to hear that Lizzie would be joining her for the half term weekend.

"You'll love my family," she assured Lizzie. "I think you will fit right in. Mom will put another bed in our room and Patricia has also invited a friend – a girl in her class called Alice, who is also a boarder. Our room will be almost like a dorm! It's a big room, so we won't be squashed at all."

"I can't wait!" said Lizzie eagerly, jumping up and down. "Thank you so much!"

All the girls in Bluebell dorm were going away for the weekend. Some were going home, but the rest were going to friends.

Matron came in to check on the packing and to see that each girl had all she would need.

"I don't want any toothbrushes left behind this

time," she said laughing. Soon the girls were ready, and they headed up to the main driveway to wait for their lifts.

"This is us!" shouted Beverley, as a huge SUV pulled up into a parking place near them. "Come on Lizzie! Here's my Mom."

All the cases were placed in the back and five girls climbed in.

"Mum, this is Lizzie Sinclair," said Beverley as soon as they were seated.

"I'm very pleased to meet you at last, Lizzie, and so happy that you could join us!" said Mrs. Cornhill smiling over her shoulder at Lizzie. "And a big hello to the rest of you! I do so love a full house. I hope you are all going to have lots of fun."

Susan Cornhill had chosen not to bring a friend home this time as she wanted to spend time horse riding with her boyfriend. She had invited him to be her partner for the final year's school dance next term. He had readily accepted, and she was so excited. She would have to spend some time too, finding a suitable dress and shoes. She wanted something extra special, and her mom had promised to take her shopping on the Monday of half term.

The Cornhills lived a fair distance from the school. It took them almost half an hour to get there. Lizzie wondered what sort of house they would have. It had to be a big one, with enough room for five children, she thought. What she saw as Mrs. Cornhill turned in at the gate, was a curved driveway, rolling lawns, bright flower borders and a lovely old golden brick double-storey house, with sparkling windows and a huge front door.

Two golden retrievers rushed down the front steps to meet them, followed by a handsome young boy with brown hair and bright blue eyes.

"That must be Brian," thought Lizzie," and oh, what a beautiful old house!"

"That's Kimble and this is Carrie", said Bev pointing to the two dogs, "Don't worry, they are very friendly, and this is Brian!" she added, giving her brother a quick hug.

"You have such a pretty garden," said Lizzie. "And I'm pleased to meet you, Brian!" She smiled at him, and he grinned back.

"There's a swimming pool in the back garden," said Bev. "We can swim if the water is warm enough."

"Oh, but I haven't brought my costume," sighed Lizzie.

"Don't worry, one of mine is sure to fit you. Come on, let's go inside."

Lizzie collected her suitcase and followed her friend up the front steps.

"I'll show you around!" offered Brian, leading the way into a very inviting entrance hall.

"We'll go up to the bedroom first and put your case down. Then I'll show you the bathroom we use," said Bev as they followed Brian, who took the stairs two at a time, with the dogs at his heels. Patricia and Alice made their way upstairs, too.

Lizzie was surprised at the size of the bedroom. It was indeed large enough for the four beds it now held. It had windows facing the driveway and front garden and was light and bright with strawberry pink bedspreads on the beds and floral curtains. There was a big carpet on the polished wooden floor. The furniture was white – white headboards on two of the beds and white bedside tables, with reading lamps. Against the far wall, were two desks, with mirrors on the wall, so that they could double for dressing tables. The chairs were white with strawberry pink covered seats.

"This is so pretty!" exclaimed Lizzie, as she looked around. Her eyes fell on a painting of flowers on the wall between the beds.

"Glad you like it. And that painting was done by Susan, she's the artist in the family!" she added. "This will be your bed," said her friend, "and this is mine, just next to it. Put your case down and we'll show you around".

Brian, who had been waiting at the door, joined them. Downstairs they went again and made their way into a very large kitchen. Lizzie was most impressed.

"We mostly eat in here," said Beverley, pointing to the big oak table that stood in the centre of the room. The kitchen windows looked onto the back garden, with tall trees on both sides and in the distance, Lizzie could see the pool. It looked most inviting, and she hoped it would be warm enough to swim.

Next Beverley and Brian took her into another big room, which she was told, was the formal dining room, and then into the living room. This was also a spacious room, with a fireplace and comfortable looking chairs and sofas. There was a baby grand piano across one corner.

"Who else plays the piano besides you?" Lizzie asked.

"Just about all of us, I think," laughed Bev. "Some better than others, and the boys both play their guitars. Susan plays the flute."

"Wow!" exclaimed Lizzie. "Do you have family concerts, then?"

"Yes, we do. It's great fun and we all sing too, especially my dad. He has a really good voice."

"I'd love to hear you," said Lizzie.

"Oh, I'm sure you will. Probably on Saturday night, if everyone's here that is."

Next, they went into the library, which was once again a warm, bright room, with bookcases along two walls and several comfortable looking chairs.

There was a cloakroom next to the library. And beyond that, Mr. Cornhill's study. He was a heart specialist and Beverley said there were lots of medical books and other medical things in there and that her dad preferred it if his children did not disturb anything, although it was not strictly out of bounds!

"So now you've seen this floor, except for the pantry and the laundry, but I've kept the best part for last," said Bev. Leading the way to a carpeted flight of stairs, which apparently led to the basement. Down they went and Lizzie couldn't believe her eyes as they entered an enormous entertainment area, which seemed to her to stretch the entire length of the house. She just stood and stared. Brian, who had followed them down, giggled.

"I love this. I love the whole house, but I do love this space!" gasped Lizzie, who had never seen anything quite like it before. "How lucky you are! TV; games of all kinds and even a snack bar at the end. If I were you Bev, I think I would live down here!"

Beverley laughed, feeling very pleased.

"This house belonged to our grandparents, you know, and they had eight children. We have five, so this space is very useful, especially when we have friends over and on rainy or very cold days. This used to be a workshop and storage area until a few years ago when my dad and Peter decided to transform it and we were all so pleased they did."

"I'll say," said Brian grinning. "Look, I've got all my Lego in here and this is my Lego table."

"What are you building now?" asked Lizzie. "I love Lego!"

"It's going to be an old castle," replied Brian, showing Lizzie a picture on a box lid.

"Oh, you've just made a friend for life!" laughed Bev. "He'll keep you busy all weekend, if you let him."

And so began Lizzie's wonderful weekend with her new friends. They watched movies in the basement with Patricia and Alice and made popcorn and pancakes, too, which they had with hot chocolate. They were able to have a swim in the pool just once before the weather turned cold again. There was a family concert on the Saturday evening and Lizzie was able to join in with some of the singing.

But all good things come to an end and far too soon it was time to return to school. Mrs. Cornhill drove the boarders back in time for them to unpack their suitcases before bedtime.

"Goodbye and thank you so much for everything." said Lizzie to Mrs. Cornhill.

Mrs. Cornhill gave her a hug. "It's been lovely having you, Lizzie," she replied. "You must come again soon."

"I would love to," said Lizzie as she waved the Cornhills goodbye. And she really meant it. She had enjoyed herself so much, that she had no time to think of her troubles at all.

CHAPTER 14

Mrs Berry's phone call

Lizzie soon settled back into the school routine after her wonderful half term with the Cornhills. She was pleased to share her experience with her other friends in the dorm. She had written all the details to her mother earlier and she was just about to get into bed on her third night back, when she was called to the telephone in Matron's office.

Quickly putting on her dressing gown and slippers once more, Lizzie hurried out of the dorm and down the passage. Matron's door was open, so Lizzie just knocked and went inside.

"Ah, there you are, Lizzie," said Matron, handing her the receiver. "I think you know the lady on the phone?"

Indeed, Lizzie did! It was Mrs. Berry.

"Hello dear," she said, "I've been to see your grandmother today and she would love to see you.

If you can arrange some time off tomorrow afternoon, I could fetch you, possibly around half past two. How does that sound?"

"I'll have to ask Miss Gorley for permission," said Lizzie, "but I am almost certain she'll say yes. Thank you, Mrs. Berry. I have to go to bed now, but I'll ask her after assembly tomorrow morning and then call you back to confirm. Will you be at home?"

"Yes, dear. I'll wait for your call. I hope you won't miss any important lessons."

"No, we have gym tomorrow afternoon, or maybe swimming if it's warm enough, so it won't matter if I'm not there."

"That's good. Sleep well, Lizzie and good night." And with that, Mrs. Berry rang off.

Matron walked Lizzie back to Bluebell dorm and wished her a good night with a warm smile. She was growing quite fond of brave young Lizzie, who was coping rather well, under very difficult circumstances. As for Lizzie herself, she was so excited at the thought of seeing her granny again. She took a while to fall asleep, but she was up bright and early the next morning, even before the rising bell, wishing the time away so that she could go to Miss Gorley's office after assembly.

Lizzie asked Beverley to go with her and the two

set off as soon as they could, after telling Miss Price that they would be a little late for their first lesson. They found Miss Gorley already seated at her desk, and when Lizzie explained what she wanted, she greeted the girl warmly.

"I've been expecting this visit, Elizabeth and of course you must go. I will telephone Mrs. Berry myself, I have her number, and I will arrange for one of the senior girls to wait with you in the driveway just before half past two, until she comes. Please be back in time for supper. I would not like you to miss the meal, as it's a long time afterwards until breakfast. And don't forget to report to Matron on your return."

"Yes, Miss Gorley, and thank you."

"Off you go now to your class. I hear only good things about you from Miss Price and I believe that despite all your troubles, you are working very well and that you have made several new friends. I am pleased about that, too, dear."

Lizzie and Beverley walked as quickly as they could to their classroom without running, which was of course, against the rules.

CHAPTER 15

The visit

Mrs. Berry arrived to collect Lizzie at half past two, as arranged. She was glad to see her waiting in the driveway, in the company of an older girl. Lizzie said goodbye to Patricia Cornhill, who had been waiting with her and climbed into the car.

On the way to the Convalescent home, where Lizzie knew her grandmother would be waiting for her, Mrs. Berry told her what to expect. Her granny was making slow progress but was not nearly ready to go home. She followed a daily routine of both physiotherapy and occupational therapy. Her injuries had been severe and the operations she had undergone had been complicated. They had taken their toll on her general health. Her mind was as sharp as ever and her attitude was positive. Everyone expected her to make a full recovery. Of course, she was worried about her son, Lizzie's dad, and looked forward to letters from her daughter-in-law, which had so far not been all that encouraging.

Lizzie was so happy to see her granny again, but she was alarmed too, as she noticed that her poor gran had lost so much weight. She decided wisely not to comment on this. Granny always said that it was rude to make personal remarks, didn't she?

They chatted for a while about Lizzie's new school. Her grandmother wanted to know all the details.

"I still can't get over how you found Oakwood all on your own, Lizzie! Your guardian angels must have been watching over you that day," remarked Mrs. Berry.

"I agree!" laughed Granny Jane.

All too soon it was time to leave, and Lizzie promised to visit again, just as soon as she could.

Mrs. Berry got Lizzie back to Oakwood just in time for supper. As instructed, Lizzie went first to report to Matron Jordan, before going into the dining room. It had been another busy and rather emotional day and Lizzie felt very tired as she ate her meal. She did not feel much like talking and was glad when she was able to go up to Bluebell dorm. Not even the thought of story time could cheer her up. She just wanted to curl up in her bed and go to sleep. Instead, she sat through another chapter of Harry Potter. She had to admit to herself that she enjoyed it very much. Matron was certainly an excellent reader.

CHAPTER 16

Lizzie receives some bad news

A few days later, Lizzie found herself once again in Miss Gorley's office. A prefect had come to fetch her just after morning break. This time when Lizzie entered the office, Miss Gorley was not smiling. In fact, she looked very grave, and Lizzie wondered what she could have done wrong. What school rule had she broken, without knowing it?

"Sit down, Elizabeth," said Miss Gorley. "I'm afraid that I have some rather serious news for you. Your grandmother wanted to tell you herself, but she was understandably upset when she phoned me, so she asked me to tell you instead. It is never easy to be the bearer of bad news." Miss Gorley came round from behind her desk, sat down next to Lizzie and took her hand.

"My dear," she began, "Your grandmother

received news this morning that her son, your father, is missing in action. That does not necessarily mean that something bad has happened to him. What it means is that, at this time, the army does not know exactly where he is. The story is that he and three other soldiers, went into a deeply forested area about five or six days ago, on a special mission and that they have not yet reported back to headquarters. In fact, there has been no word from any of them at all. A search party has now been sent out and everything will be done in order to find these men. We will just have to pray that they will soon be found, and in good health. I don't want you to worry too much, but your grandmother wanted you to know, all the same. We must hope for the best, mustn't we? Your mother is doing all she can to help. She will keep us all informed.

As it is now very nearly the end of term, we will have to see what arrangements can be made for you for the holidays, dear. Perhaps you could go home with Beverley again? I do know that the Cornhills enjoyed having you to stay over half term. Just be as brave as you can. That is all you can do."

Lizzie sat quite still in her chair. Miss Gorley was still holding her hand. Then suddenly her small shoulders began to shake a little and she gave a mournful sob.

"Oh, Miss Gorley, I just knew something awful would happen. I begged them not to go. Well, Daddy had to because it is his job, but Mummy didn't really have to, did she? But perhaps she will be able to help with the search. What do you think?"

"They will all do whatever is possible, you can be assured of that. Let's hope that all four men are found quickly and in good health. Now, would you like to go back to your class, or would you prefer some time to yourself, perhaps in the garden? It's a lovely day to be outside.

We'll have some tea first, I think, if you would just ring that little bell over there. That goes through to the kitchen and someone there will know that I need a tray of tea and biscuits! It won't take long, you'll see. In the meantime, you can tell me how you found your grandmother, the other day. I am sure she was very pleased to see you."

So Lizzie told Miss Gorley all about her visit to the convalescent home and just as she finished, there was a knock on the door. The tea tray had arrived!

Afterwards, Lizzie made her way back to her classroom. She really did not want to be alone, and she also did not want to miss her art lesson either. She would try not to cry. She had made up her mind over tea. What was the use of that? What she would do, was ask her friend Beverley if her family had any plans for the holidays. That way, Beverley was certain to ask her the same question and she would tell her the bad news then. She just wished she could talk to her granny. She would ask Matron if she could call her after supper. Perhaps Matron would have heard the news herself by then.

Lizzie would be brave. She would be positive, as Miss Gorley had said, and she would try to comfort her granny. Yes, her beloved father was lost or missing, but he was not alone. He was with three other men, strong soldiers. They would surely be able to find their way back out of that forest, Lizzie reasoned, trying to comfort herself, as she made her way back to join the rest of her class.

She arrived just as they were lining up to go to the art room. Beverley greeted Lizzie warmly and they walked down together. There was no talking allowed in the corridors to the art room and for once Lizzie was very grateful for that rule. It gave her a little more time to settle her thoughts. She sensed though, that Beverley would want to know why she had been called to Miss Gorley's office yet again. Lizzie decided that she would answer only partly and say that it had to do with her grandmother, and that she, Lizzie was hoping to phone her after their supper.

CHAPTER 17

Lizzie's phone call

When Lizzie went to Matron's office after supper, she found that Matron did indeed know what Lizzie thought of as "the bad news." In her usual kindly way, Matron gave her a hug and when Lizzie asked if she could phone her grandmother, Matron readily agreed and in fact, she dialed the number herself and asked to be put through to Mrs. Sinclair. There was a brief pause and then Matron handed the phone to Lizzie.

"Hello Granny, it's me, Lizzie. I had to speak to you to see if you are all right. You mustn't worry about Daddy. I just know he'll be fine, and he wouldn't like us to worry. You know what he always says, don't you? That worrying does nobody any good. He'd say that to me sometimes if I was anxious about a test, or something. So please, don't worry Gran."

"My dear child, you are so brave and sensible for your age! Of course, I will try not to worry, but as the mother of a soldier, I always knew that going into battle in a strange country would be dangerous. But your own mother is very resourceful and brave, too, and she will not rest until those four soldiers have been found. Maybe they will all be sent home then. Wouldn't that be wonderful?"

"Yes, it would. I do hope so. I'll say good night now, Granny. I will try to visit you again as soon as I can. I'm sure Miss Gorley will give me permission. She's very kind, you know. In fact, everyone here is kind. I haven't yet met one mean person. This is the very best school, Gran. I do love it here! Good night!"

"Good night, Lizzie. Thank you for calling. I will sleep much more easily now that I have spoken to you."

Lizzie handed the receiver back to Matron and thanked her for the call.

"Good night, Elizabeth. I hope you sleep well," said Matron, with a smile.

Lizzie hurried back to the dorm to prepare for bed. Mary Johnson watched her and noticed that Lizzie was quieter than usual. Something was definitely worrying her new little friend.

"Lizzie is everything all right?" she asked quietly, so as not to alert the other girls. "Is your Grandmother okay?"

"Yes, I've just spoken to her, Mary. That's what I've been doing in Matron's office. I'll go and see her again as soon as I can. Good night, Mary," replied Lizzie, quickly ending the conversation. She did not want to discuss her problems with anyone just yet and she didn't want any sympathy, either, because that might just make her cry. So, getting into bed, she clutched her Teddy bear close to her and closed her eyes. She hoped she would fall asleep quickly.

However, Lizzie slept restlessly that night. She kept waking up and wondering where her father was and if perhaps, he had been found. She wondered too, where her mother was, and when she would hear from her again.

At last, she heard the rising bell, and she was thankful that the night was over. She had hardly eaten any supper the night before and despite all her troubles, Lizzie found that she was hungry. She washed and dressed quickly, made her bed and was ready a full five minutes before the breakfast bell. Mary watched her without saying anything. She could tell that poor Lizzie had something bothering her. What it was, Mary had no way of guessing.

“She’ll tell me when she’s ready,” she thought, “or maybe not.” Mary was not an inquisitive child by nature. With that she joined the others as they made their way downstairs to the dining room.

The usual morning chatter at the table, helped to keep Lizzie’s mind off her troubles, especially as she listened to a tale that Rosie Bishop was telling.

CHAPTER 18

Beverley's invitation

A few days later, Beverley found Lizzie sitting alone on a bench under a big oak tree. She was sitting very still and as Beverley approached her, she did not move. She remained staring off into the distance, as if lost in thought. Beverley sat down beside her friend and waited quietly. Eventually Lizzie said,

"Bev, what are your plans for the hols? Are you and your family going away?"

"No," replied Beverley. "We'll be at home. Peter doesn't have time off from his university and Susan is studying for her final school exams. Patricia is having Alice to stay for a week and Brian is going to his friend James, who lives on a farm. What are your plans, Lizzie? Do you have any yet?"

"No," said Lizzie rather sadly. "Granny is not yet strong enough to go home and Miss Gorley said that

I could probably stay on here, unless my uncle comes to fetch me. I don't think he will, because it is a very long way for him to make the trip up and down in just three weeks. He's my mother's younger brother, you know, and he and my aunt have three young children. They don't live anywhere near where we live, and so we don't see then very often. I hardly know my cousins."

Beverley thought for a bit and then she jumped up saying "I'll ask Mom this afternoon if you can come to us! I'm sure she'll say yes, because otherwise I'll be very much on my own. I'm sure Miss Gorley will be happy for you, too. Wait till tomorrow and then we'll go together and ask her. Oh, Lizzie, we'll have so much fun! Just think! Three whole weeks…"

But Lizzie did not respond as joyfully as Beverley had thought she would. Although she was relieved, she just sat staring off into the distance again. Come to think of it, thought Beverley, Lizzie had been very quiet and rather dreamy, the last few days.

"Aren't you feeling well, Liz?" she asked kindly. "Would you like me to take you up to Matron?"

"No, I'm not ill, don't worry, Bev. I'd love to come home with you for the hols., it's just …" and with that poor Lizzie burst into tears. She had been holding back and now she just couldn't anymore.

"My goodness," said Bev in alarm, "Are you homesick, Liz?"

"In a way," sobbed Lizzie. "But it is more than that…"

"Do you want to talk about it?"

"I didn't, I've been trying hard not to," said Lizzie, wiping her nose with a tissue, "but now perhaps I will. But Bev, you mustn't tell anyone, except your mom. Promise? Absolutely no one here at school."

"Okay, I promise," said Beverley solemnly, suddenly thinking that something awful must have happened.

"Well," started Lizzie between sniffs, "You know my dad is a soldier in the army?" Bev nodded, "Miss Gorley told me a few days ago that it has been reported that he and three other soldiers are missing. They went into a thick forest a while ago, I'm not sure when, exactly, and no one has seen them since. They just didn't come out again and now search parties have been sent in to look for them."

"Oh, Lizzie, how absolutely dreadful," whispered Beverley, putting her arm around her friend. "So that's why you've been so quiet."

"Yes," said Lizzie with a sob. "That's why, but I'm glad now that my mother is there, because she will demand that they all keep looking. She's very determined, you know and very tough. She has to be, as a war correspondent. That means that she writes about what is happening, for newspapers and magazines. Oh, I do so wish that everyone would just stop fighting and wanting things that they haven't got, like other people's land. IT IS SO STUPID!" Lizzie jumped up angrily.

"Yes, it is, isn't it? But there have always been wars, Lizzie," remarked Bev wisely. "Men just love fighting for power, and they teach young children about it too, with all the war games they love to play, and toy guns and things. I love history, so I've read a lot and I know. You must have learnt about some of the wars too, but that doesn't make it any easier for you now, does it?"

Lizzie shook her head, thinking that if only she could get a letter from her mother today, things might be better.

A bell rang in the distance.

"Come on," said Bev. "You don't want to miss your supper, and I have to run for the last bus. I'll ask Mom about the holidays, but I know she'll say yes. Come on, Lizzie!" She tugged her friend's hand, "Let's run over to the quad together. I left my backpack on the wall there when I came to look for you."

They ran off together and hugged each other goodbye when they reached the quad.

"Your secret's safe with me, Lizzie. Do try to be positive, if you can, and get a good night's sleep. I think you could do with one!" And with that, Beverley rushed off to catch the last school bus home.

Lizzie wandered listlessly over to the junior dining room. She did not feel particularly hungry, but she knew better than to try to miss a meal. Maybe tomorrow would bring better news. She hoped so, with all her heart. It least she wouldn't worry about holiday plans tonight. She felt quite sure that kind Mrs. Cornhill would say yes.

CHAPTER 19

Holiday plans

Beverley rushed into the classroom the next day, full of excitement. Lizzie was standing gloomily next to her desk, waiting for the bell to ring for assembly. She had spent another restless night, but she looked up as her friend arrived and smiled weakly.

"Lizzie, Lizzie, mom said yes! You are to spend the whole hols with us! Isn't that super? We have so much to think of and plan! Mom's going to phone Miss Gorley later today, so you don't have to worry!"

"Thank you so much!" said Lizzie cheering up a little. "That's really kind of your mom."

"Yes, and if there is any news of you know what, Miss Gorley will be able to find you, so that's good and mom said that she will gladly take you to visit your granny, she said so. In fact, it was her idea. "Lizzie will want to visit her grandmother often," is what she said, "and we'll take her!"

Lizzie was so relieved. That meant she didn't have to ask, herself. She did not like asking favours of others, especially as she was to be a guest in their very busy household. How kind Mrs. Cornhill was, and how lucky it was that Bev was now her best friend. She decided that she would tell Mary Johnson tonight, so that she would stop looking at her in her questioning, but caring way. Dear little Mary! Lizzie felt very lucky to be sleeping in the bed next to her and not next to Sarah Potts and her practical jokes, or even Rosie Bishop, or Nosey Rosie, as she was sometimes called, because she asked so many personal questions and wanted to know everyone's business. Mary was quiet and kind and Lizzie counted her as a very good friend.

Just before first break, there was a knock at the classroom door and an older girl walked in with a message. Lizzie was please to go directly to Miss Gorley's office at the beginning of break.

All the girls turned to look at Lizzie, who blushed and looked down at the book open on her desk. The class all wanted to know why Elizabeth Sinclair was so often called to see Miss Gorley. To the others it was a mystery, for Lizzie had not confided in anyone, except most recently, Beverley.

"Now girls," said Miss Price firmly. Please turn your attention back to your work for the last five minutes of this lesson. I can assure you that Lizzie is not in any trouble, for those of you who are curious!"

The girls looked down at their books again. Bev smiled encouragingly across the aisle at Lizzie, hoping that today's meeting was about the holidays, as there was only one week left of term.

Miss Price let Lizzie out of class just before the break bell, so that she would still have time for her tea after her meeting with the principal.

Lizzie hurried to the office and knocked at the door. She no longer had to be escorted, as she knew her way well. She was greeted by Miss Gorley's cheerful "Come in!"

"Ah yes! I've been expecting you, Lizzie," said Miss Gorley. "Do sit down. This won't take long. I've had a call from Mrs. Cornhill, who has invited you to spend the holidays with their family. I readily gave my consent. I think it will be a very good break for you, dear, as you get on so well with Beverley. ALSO, I will be able to reach you if there is any more news about your father. I am not going away, you see. Morningside Cottage is my home here, as you know. Your grandmother has been informed and is most happy and relieved about the arrangements. Any letters that might arrive for you, will be sent on immediately, to the Cornhills.

Matron will help you to pack. So, you see, Elizabeth, you have nothing to worry about from this end, although I am sure you are anxious about your father, and that is only to be expected. There is nothing you can do about that, except to keep him in your thoughts and prayers. I want you to have fun with your friends. I've a strong feeling that all will be well in the end."

Without warning, Lizzie began to cry. "I'm sorry," she said between sobs. "Everyone is so kind, that's all. Thank you, Miss Gorley. May I go now?"

"Yes dear, you may, but go to the cloakroom first and wash your face. Then go and enjoy your tea. I think it's peanut butter sandwiches and fresh orange juice today." Miss Gorley walked over to the door and opened it for Lizzie, who thanked her again as she hurried off to the cloakroom.

CHAPTER 20

Lizzie confides in Mary Johnson

The last days of term went by very quickly, and before she knew it, the time had come to pack her suitcase for the holidays. As she retrieved her case from the box room, Mary asked her where she was going. She had been a kind and patient friend and had not questioned Lizzie at all.

"I'm spending the holidays with the Cornhills," she said, "My granny is still in the convalescent home, Mary, where she has to do a lot of exercises every day to make her strong again. She probably won't be going home to her house for at least another month. My uncle and aunt live such a long way away, so Beverley has invited me and that's where I'm going!"

"So your parents are not back yet either?"

"No, they're not," replied Lizzie, trying hard not

to cry.

"Why, whatever is the matter, Lizzie?" asked observant little Mary. "Do you miss them so very much?"

"Yes, I do, but it is not that…it's just…Oh, I might as well tell you Mary, but please, please don't tell anyone else, will you? You see, my father is missing, Mary. He and three other soldiers went into a big forest for some reason which I haven't been told, and now they can't be found. Well, not as far as I know, anyway. That's why I've been so quiet. But you won't tell the others, will you? I don't want anyone to make a fuss."

"Oh, Lizzie, how awful for you! Of course, I won't tell anyone else. I'm just so sad for you but I think they will find him soon and then perhaps both your parents will come home. Only, if they do, will you have to leave Oakwood, do you think? I do hope not."

"I really don't know what will happen, but I like being here and I don't want to leave. I have no brothers or sisters and so at home, I'm on my own a lot. It's much more fun being here amongst all of you. There's something nice to do all the time and I've made friends. I like sleeping in the bed next to yours, Mary. Perhaps I will be able to stay… I hope so, anyway."

Matron arrived at that moment to supervise the packing, so Mary simply smiled at Lizzie and said, "I hope so too, Lizzie."

The suitcases were soon packed and ready and the girls carried them out into the passage outside their dorm. Mary and Lizzie made their way together down to the dining room for lunch, before the final assembly, which was really just for Miss Gorley to say goodbye to them all and to wish them well for the holidays on behalf of all the staff.

Beverley went with Lizzie to collect her suitcase, hat and coat and teddy bear, before making their way up to the top driveway, where they spotted Mrs. Cornhill already waiting for them beside her car.

Goodbyes were shouted to all their friends, as Lizzie, Beverley, Patricia, Susan, and Alice all climbed into the car and buckled up for the ride home.

"Wow" said Bev "At last! Three weeks of fun! We're going to have a great time Lizzie, wait and see!"

Lizzie smiled at her friend, but her mind was on other things. There had not been a letter from her mother for weeks and she was very worried. It was hard for her to think of having fun, with all that she had on her mind. However, she was determined not to be a wet blanket, as she had heard others say, and she would not spoil these holidays for her kind friend. Beverley had been so supportive and had not asked Lizzie any painful questions since she, Lizzie, had told her about her father being missing.

Lizzie settled back quietly in her seat in the car and tried to put her troubles out of her mind. Mrs. Cornhill had promised her a visit to her grandmother the next day. She would think of that, instead. She listened to the happy chatter of her friends, as they made plans for the coming days.

Their journey was soon over, and Bev helped Lizzie carry all her belongings upstairs to her bedroom.

"I've made place for your clothes here in these drawers, Liz," she said kindly "and you can hang your dresses in my closet. You have the same bed as last time," she added, flopping down onto her own. "Gosh, I'm so glad you are here! Let me help you put away your things and then we can go downstairs. It's warm enough today for a swim. Did you bring your costume?"

"Yes," laughed Lizzie, remembering half term weekend when she had borrowed one of Bev's. She placed her bear on her bed. "A swim would be good. Should we change in here?" The girls were still in their school uniforms.

"Yes, just throw all your clothes in this washing

basket," replied Bev, pointing to a large white basket in the corner of the room. "We'll do our laundry while we are swimming and then when it's dry, we can put it all away for three whole weeks! Oh, I haven't shown you our laundry room yet, have I? It's just off the kitchen, next to the pantry."

Mrs. Cornhill had made a delicious supper for everyone. Bev and Liz were very hungry after their long swim and both girls asked for second helpings. Later, they joined Patricia and Alice in the den, to watch a movie, but all agreed that they felt too full for popcorn!

"Don't stay up too late, Bev and Liz, we've a busy day tomorrow." Mrs. Cornhill had called, as they made their way downstairs, "I've a surprise for you in the morning, and in the afternoon, Lizzie, we'll visit your grandmother. She will probably be waiting anxiously to see you and I am really looking forward to meeting her, too."

CHAPTER 21

The surprise

The girls were up very early the next morning. They could hardly wait to find out more about the surprise, but Mrs. Cornhill said, with a smile,

"You'll just have to wait and see!"

As soon as breakfast was over, Beverley and Lizzie were told to go out to Mrs. Cornhill's car, and off they went! They were excited and kept looking at each other and grinning, but they knew better than to pester Mrs. Cornhill with any further questions. They would indeed, just have to wait.

After about fifteen minutes, the girls noticed that they were driving out of the city and shortly after that, Mrs. Cornhill pulled off the main highway and onto a much smaller, tree lined road.

"Oh, now I know where we are!" cried Beverley excitedly. "This is the way to the Parkers' farm, isn't it mom? Are we going to visit your friend Bianca?"

"That's right, Bev, we are," laughed her mother, "but that isn't really the surprise. Lizzie, Bianca Parker and I went to school together at Oakwood and we've remained the best of friends ever since." Explained Mrs. Cornhill, "Bianca married Tom Parker and they settled on the farm we are going to. They grow the most wonderful fruit, apples; plums; pears and cherries, in the right seasons. You'll see for yourself. They have three sons, Liam, Donald, and Cedric, but I am not sure if you will meet any of them today."

They were approaching a gravel driveway and after a few minutes, Lizzie caught sight of a beautiful farmhouse, surrounded by lawns, flower beds and shrubs. The house itself was a big single-storey one and it seemed to stretch out on both sides of a bright blue front door.

"Oh, that's amazing!" Lizzie blurted out, knowing immediately that this was a very welcoming place and that she was going to love being here.

Mrs. Parker must have been waiting for them, because as the car crunched its way up the driveway, she flung open the blue door, ran down the steps and stood waving to them.

"Jill, hello, hello!" she called, her voice drifting through the open windows of the car. "You're in very good time. It is lovely to see you. I've got fresh lemonade and snacks waiting for you in the kitchen. You must be parched; it is such a hot day!"

"Thanks, B.," Jill Cornhill shouted back as she parked and got out of the car. The two women hugged each other, and Lizzie was introduced. "Lemonade would be most welcome, but I am not sure that we have room for any eats. It seems as if we have only just had breakfast!"

Bianca Parker led the way through a spacious hallway and into an enormous farm style kitchen. It was definitely the biggest kitchen Lizzie had ever seen, not counting the school kitchen, which she had caught a glimpse of once, a few weeks ago. The floor was tiled and looked spotless. Down the centre of the room was a modern "island", with huge stainless-steel sinks at one end. Arranged around the other end were eight tall stools. Lizzie thought that the family probably had their meals there.

Set out on a side counter, Bianca pointed to a big jug of lemonade and several plates of homemade biscuits, and a basket of blueberry muffins, that had probably just come out of the oven. Lizzie and Beverley eyed each other and could hardly wait to be invited to tuck in! Mrs. Parker poured out the lemonade as they filled their plates and sat down on the stools. Lizzie wondered if this was the surprise. If it was, it was certainly a good one, she thought.

However, suddenly the back door opened, and a very tall, very good-looking man strode in, removing his hat.

"Hello all!" He beamed, glancing round at everyone. "And who do we have here?" he asked, smiling warmly at Lizzie.

"I'm Elizabeth Sinclair, but most people call me Liz or Lizzie", she replied.

"I'm Tom Parker, and I'm very pleased to meet you, Lizzie," he replied formally, but he came forward and gave her a warm hug.

"Are you girls ready? Had enough to eat?" The two girls nodded. "Good, good, let's go then." He said, quickly gulping down a glass of lemonade, and picking up a muffin, he led the way out of the back door. Putting on his hat, he finished the muffin in a few bites. Poor Lizzie thought of her own father and wondered, as she did many times a day, if he and the other men had been found. She didn't say anything to anyone, not even to Bev, but her heart ached so often as she held back her tears.

Now they were heading towards a large barn. Could the surprise be in there? She hoped so, but she could not imagine what it might be. So many things might be kept in a big barn like that.

Mr. Parker pushed open the big door and beckoned for the girls to follow him. Although there were windows high up along one side, it was fairly dark inside. He flipped a switch and lights went on all the way down the length of the barn.

"Over here," he said, as he strode down between some farm equipment and a large tractor. He stopped suddenly and beckoned to them again. And there, on a pile of old sacks, was a mother cat and four sweet little kittens!

"Your mother told me you've been wanting a kitten, Beverley, and she has agreed that you may have one of these when they are ready to leave their mother. She's our house cat, Molly, and she has a very sweet and loving nature. I'm quite sure her kittens will be just as loving. What do you say? Would you like to choose one now?"

"Oh, my goodness!" exclaimed Beverley, "What a wonderful surprise! I could never have guessed. I thought the outing and the eats was the surprise. How old are the kittens, Tom?"

"They were eight weeks old yesterday, so they will be ready to leave their mother before the end of your holidays, I should think," he replied.

"May I touch them?" asked Bev.

"Certainly, I'm sure Molly won't mind, seeing

that I'm here with you."

"Oh, I just love all of them, how am I going to choose? What do you think, Lizzie, which one would you pick?"

"They are very sweet – are they boys or girls?" replied Lizzie.

Mr. Parker said, "Three girls and one boy. I think you ought to pick a girl, Beverley."

"Yes, I think so, too. Please show me a little girl," said Bev. Mr. Parker picked out a black kitten with white front paws and lovely blue eyes.

"Here you are," he said, "How do you like this one?"

"Bev held the tiny kitten in her cupped hands. "I love her! Isn't she just the sweetest little thing you've ever seen, Lizzie!"

"She's adorable," said Lizzie, her eyes shining.

"Here, you can hold her for a bit, too," said Bev, handing the kitten over to her.

The mother cat, Molly, looked on, an anxious expression in her eyes. Mr. Parker knelt down and stroked her reassuringly until she began to purr loudly.

"Well, if you like that one, Bev, I'll remember her, and you can come and collect her at the end of next week. I'll ask the vet to drop by and check them all out beforehand. He'll give us some feeding instructions, too. "

"Oh, thank you so much!" said Bev, handing the kitten back to Mr. Parker, who placed her very carefully back next to her mother.

They left the barn and Bev and Liz ran back towards the house.

"Mom, Mom," shouted Bev, excitedly, as they burst into the kitchen. "That was the very best surprise ever! I'm to have a kitten all of my own, in a week's time! Thank you soooo much!" She run up to her mother and gave her a tight hug.

Jill Cornhill hugged her back and smiled. "That kitten will be your responsibility, Bev. I know you will take good care of her. In the meantime, we'll go to the Pet Shop and get a bed and other supplies for her. I am quite sure though, that in the end, she will land up sleeping on your bed!" she laughed.

"Probably," sighed Bev, who was flushed with excitement. Lizzie was very happy for her friend, too.

"The two of you can go off and explore, if you like," said Bianca Parker, "I'd like to chat to your mom a little longer, if you don't mind, Bev. I believe that you have an important arrangement this afternoon and won't be staying for lunch. Give us another hour together, dears," she added, as Bev and Liz headed for the back door again.

On the drive home, Bev was still bubbling over with excitement. What a wonderful surprise that had been.

"You'll have to visit us often, Liz," she said, "so you can watch the kitten grow."

"Well, after this, only at half term, Bev," replied Lizzie.

"Have you thought of a name for her yet?" asked her mother.

"Not yet, but I will. Liz will help, too, won't you?" replied Bev generously.

CHAPTER 22

The afternoon visit

After a quick sandwich lunch, Liz and Bev tidied themselves and were back in Mrs. Cornhill's car by two thirty. Visiting hours began at three o'clock. But unlike the hospital, they could stay longer than an hour, if Mrs. Sinclair was not too tired. Lizzie could hardly wait to see her grandmother and to introduce her friends.

They arrived at the Home in very good time and were surprised to see that it was a lovely sprawling house, set in well- kept grounds. The house itself had a wide covered verandah stretching the length of the building, with chairs and tables and a few benches spaced out along it. It all looked very inviting.

Mrs. Cornhill led the way towards the large open double doors. They found themselves in an entrance hall, devoid of furniture, except for a table with a fresh flower arrangement on it, and two chairs. There were no rugs or carpets on the polished wooden floor, to make it easy for wheelchairs to come and go and those with other walking aids, would be able to move about freely. A door on the left was marked RECEPTION. Mrs. Cornhill knocked and entered.

"Good afternoon," she said to a lady behind the desk. "We're here to visit Mrs. Sinclair."

"Ah yes," smiled the receptionist. She was dressed in a smart white blouse and navy-blue skirt. A badge on her blouse read "Ellen Hayward."

She stood up. "I'll take you to her," she said, smiling. She was a tall woman and slim, with short brown hair and dark brown eyes. Lizzie liked her at once.

Ellen Hayward led the way down a passage to the right of the front door, to room number 8 and a sign which read "Mrs. Jane Sinclair". She knocked and entered.

"Visitors for you Mrs. Sinclair," she said brightly, "would you like to stay in here, or would you prefer the verandah – there is no one else there at the moment."

"Outside would be lovely, Ellen," replied Mrs. Sinclair, "Just as soon as I've greeted my guests!"

Introductions were made and Lizzie hugged her granny tightly.

A nurse appeared to help Mrs. Sinclair walk to the verandah. She settled her in a comfortable armchair and arranged an extra cushion behind her back. The others carried chairs over. Mrs. Cornhill and Beverley sat down facing Mrs. Sinclair and Lizzie sat beside her, so as to hold her hand. It was so good to be with her grandmother again. The conversation flowed easily. Mrs. Cornhill said what an absolute pleasure it was to have Lizzie with them for the holidays. She also asked whether she would be staying on at Oakwood. Mrs. Sinclair explained the situation to her and said that she very much hoped that would be the case.

"I hope so too" added Lizzie. "I love it there and I don't ever want to go to another school." Mrs. Cornhill smiled at her warmly. "We all love Oakwood, don't we Bev?"

Bev agreed. "Most definitely," she said, "It's the best school ever!"

All too soon it was time to leave. They had enjoyed their tea and the delicious cake that was served with it, but they could see that Mrs. Sinclair was tired and needed to return to her room, to put her feet up for a while.

Mrs. Cornhill promised that she would bring

Lizzie to visit again in a few days and with that, they said their goodbyes, just as a nurse arrived to help Mrs. Sinclair back to her room.

"I'll phone you every day, Granny," Lizzie promised as she waved goodbye.

"I'll look forward to that, dear." Her grandmother replied, as she waved back.

CHAPTER 23

A surprise phone call

A few days later Liz and Bev were down at the pool when Mrs. Cornhill called,

"Telephone for you Lizzie!"

Lizzie grabbed her towel and ran as fast as she could to the back door.

"You can take the call in here, Lizzie," said Mrs. Cornhill, handing Lizzie the receiver.

"Hello?" said Lizzie.

"Hello, dear," answered her grandmother. "I just wanted to tell you as soon as I got the news. Your Aunt Claudia is arriving on Sunday!" She and your uncle Michael have just returned from a three-month tour of game reserves in Africa. You remember that they are both wildlife photographers?"

"Yes, I think I do."

"Well, as soon as they got back to their home in Portugal, Claudia called me. I'd written to her to tell her about my accident, but she only got the letter once they were home. Of course, she has so much to attend to, having been away for so long, but she immediately booked a flight here and will be with us for a week. Unfortunately, Mike won't be able to come this time, but they hope to visit again later, once I am home."

"Oh, that's wonderful, Gran, did you tell her about Dad?"

"Of course I did. I had also written to them about it. Claudia was most upset, as can be expected."

Lizzie gulped back her tears and managed to croak a weak "Yes, I'm sure." She wanted to be strong for her grandmother, but it was hard when she was hurting so much herself.

"Mrs. Berry is going to open up the house and put in some supplies for Claudia. She'll be staying there. She said she will take a taxi from the airport. No need to hire a car when my car is in the garage and needs to have a good run. Sheila Berry will bring her to me as soon as she arrives. Perhaps Mrs. Cornhill will be able to bring you, too. That will be this Sunday afternoon, I expect."

"I'll ask her," promised Lizzie "and I'll phone you tonight."

"That will be good dear, goodbye then. Have fun with your friends!" and with that, Mrs. Sinclair put down the receiver.

Lizzie told Mrs. Cornhill the news and she readily agreed to take Lizzie to the Convalescent Home on Sunday afternoon.

"It will be a pleasure. Don't worry, Lizzie. I had actually planned to do just that, anyway. I would very much like to meet your aunt, too. I would love to hear something of her adventures in Africa. I have never been there, but I would love to visit the Victoria Falls, one day and at least one Game Reserve. That's been on our family's bucket list for a while!"

And with that, Lizzie ran back down to the pool, to tell Bev and Patricia her good news.

CHAPTER 24

Mrs Sinclair receives a message

Mrs. Sinclair was enjoying the warm sunshine on the verandah when a nurse approached her.

"There's been a faxed message for you to the office, Mrs. Sinclair," she said, "I've brought it over for you."

Mrs. Sinclair took the piece of paper. The message was from her daughter in law, Andrea. It read:

JOHN AND CO. FOUND!
IN MILITARY HOSPITAL FOR
TREATMENT AND OBSERVATION.
WILL CONTACT YOU AGAIN
AS SOON AS POSSIBLE.
MUCH LOVE TO YOU AND LIZ.
Andrea.

"Oh!" cried Mrs. Sinclair once she had read the message. "I must go back to my room at once. I need to make several phone calls."

The nurse helped her back to her room, where she immediately called Lizzie first.

Lizzie burst into tears of joy and relief. "I just knew he'd be found," she said. "Oh Gran, do you think they'll come home soon?"

"I do hope so, dear, but that will depend on what medical treatment your dad needs. We will just have to wait patiently for your mother's next message."

Lizzie rushed to tell Mrs. Cornhill and her friends.

"May I call Miss Gorley? Do you think that she will mind a call from a student during the holidays?"

"I think Miss Gorley will be pleased to get your call, Lizzie. She's been worried too, you know. I'll get the number for you."

So Lizzie told Miss Gorley all she knew, and about her aunt's visit. Miss Gorley was very pleased and said so warmly.

"Now you will really be able to enjoy the rest of the holidays," she added.

"I will," replied Lizzie. "Thank you for everything, Miss Gorley and I hope you are enjoying your holidays, too."

Miss Gorley laughed. “Thank you dear, and goodbye for now.”

It was a much happier Lizzie who skipped off to tell her friends her good news.

Beverley was equally excited and jumped up to hug her friend. “I knew it, I knew it! I just knew it would be okay in the end, Liz. Now what shall we do to celebrate?”

Just then Mrs. Cornhill joined them. “Have you ever been ice-skating, Liz?” she asked. Lizzie shook her head.

“There’s a lovely ice rink quite near here. How would you like to spend a few hours there, girls?”

“Oh great!” replied Bev. “I love ice skating.”

“Bev’s quite good at it, Lizzie and if you haven’t done it before, I’m sure you’ll learn very quickly. We’ll go straight after lunch.”

The girls looked at each other excitedly.

“Thanks Mom,” said Bev. “That’s just what we feel like doing – it will be the perfect celebration for Lizzie.”

“But I don’t have any skates.” Said Lizzie, a worried expression on her face.

“Not to worry, we’ll hire them there, they have loads of skates in all sizes,” replied Mrs. Cornhill.

The ice-rink seemed very large to Lizzie. It was inside a very big building. Lizzie was surprised to see how busy it was. There were just as many boys as well as girls, on the ice already. They stood and watched for a few minutes.

"Come on," said Bev. "Let's get you some skates."

Mrs. Cornhill showed Lizzie where to go to get fitted. Lizzie was surprised to see that she was going to skate with them.

"I've been skating ever since the rink opened, when I was about twelve, I think. I thought I would help you, Liz, seeing it's your first time."

"Thank you," said Liz, feeling rather relieved.

They all put on their boots and while Lizzie staggered to the side of the rink, she saw that Mrs. Cornhill and Bev moved confidently.

"Come on Liz," said Bev, as her friend hesitated at the edge. "You'll soon get the hang of it!" She took her friend's hand and Mrs. Cornhill took the other.

All three of them stepped onto the ice. "OOOH!" said Liz, "It's so slippery!"

"It's ice!" laughed Bev. "Just hold on tight." They pushed away from the side and with Liz in the middle, they skated away. Lizzie felt her legs wobble a bit, but she was determined to learn quickly. Round they went, keeping fairly close to the wooden barrier. Lizzie soon began to relax a little.

"This IS fun," she said.

The afternoon flew by. Lizzie loved every minute of it, even the few falls she had. The music was cheerful, and everyone seemed so happy.

"Let's get some hot chocolate before we go," said Mrs. Cornhill, pointing to the refreshment kiosk. "We'll return Liz's skates first."

The hot chocolate was delicious and came with a choice of whipped cream or marshmallows to put on top. The girls decided to have both.

"That was so much fun, Mrs. Cornhill, thank you!" said Lizzie as she sipped her drink and watched the other skaters on the rink.

"May we come again, before the end of the hols?" asked Bev.

"I don't see why not," replied Mrs. Cornhill, "I've enjoyed myself too, and perhaps Pat would like to join us next time, Alice, too if she is still with us."

CHAPTER 25

A shopping spree

"Tom Parker called last night to say that the vet has been, and your kitten is ready to come home, Bev. But first we have a little shopping to do. I suggest that we go immediately after breakfast, come home, and set everything up, probably in your room, if you like, and then we'll head out for the farm. What do you say?"

"That's perfect! Thanks so much Mom. I know the kitten must be in just one room at first, Lizzie and I have been doing a little research. I also know that cats don't like their litter box to be near their food, so I've been wondering how to manage that."

"Good point," said her mother. "Let's think about it shall we? We'll have to ask Pat as she shares the room with you. Let's go and find her."

Patricia and her friend Alice were in the den.

“Alice has a cat of her own,” said Pat. “What do you suggest?” asked Pat of her friend, once she was told the news.

“Well, I’ve had my cat for five years and now she mostly sleeps on my bed, when I’m there, but Mom started her off in the spare room. She was quite fine there because we took a towel with us when we went to collect her, and I remember the mother cat’s owner wiped the towel all over the mother and the other two kittens and then put the towel in the carrier. She curled up on that on the way home. She slept on it in her bed, too and seemed quite happy, because she could smell her family. It’s important for you to keep the kitten away from Kimble and Carrie for a while, too.”

“I can see that you’re going to be a great help to us, Alice. Do you and Pat want to come to the farm with us later?”

“No,” replied Alice, “I think too many people might frighten the kitten in the beginning. I’ll help you set up the space for her before you go, if that’s okay?”

“That would be perfect,” replied Mrs. Cornhill. “I’m a dog person, myself and I’ve never had a cat. I think the small room next to the bathroom upstairs, will be a good place for her. There are fewer places for her to hide in there and not much for her to destroy! Your bedroom might be a bit overwhelming for her Bev, whilst she is still so little, seeing that so far, she has only seen the inside of the barn, and she has had her mother to look out for her in there."

"I think so too," said Pat and Bev readily agreed with her.

"Tom told me what food to buy, as recommended by the vet, and I've made a list of all the other items you'll need, Bev. You do realise that the kitten will be your responsibility, don't you?" Her mother reminded her.

"Oh, don't worry, Bev, we'll all help," said Pat, "But you'll be her main carer."

After breakfast Mrs. Cornhill drove Bev and Lizzie to the big pet store they had noticed on their way to visit Mrs. Sinclair.

"Let's ask for some help," said Mrs. Cornhill, list in hand, as they went inside.

A tall, kind looking man came towards them at that moment and before Mrs. Cornhill could ask, he offered his assistance. Mrs. Cornhill handed him her list.

"We are going to collect a kitten for my daughter, here, our very first cat. We have two dogs," said Mrs. Cornhill.

"I'm Graham," said the man looking at the list

and smiling. “Do follow me, we’ll put all this together in no time. Which of you two girls is the new owner? We have quite a wide variety of items here, you will have to make several choices.”

Bev stepped forward eagerly and Graham smiled at her. They walked together towards the back of the shop where Bev lost no time in choosing a carrier; a bed; food and water bowls; food; cat litter and a special box for it, and last of all, a scratching post.

“Now for some toys. You ought to have some of those.” Graham said, pointing to row upon row of toys of all kinds. Bev chose three of the smaller ones.

“We can always come back for more, when the kitten is tired of these,” she said to Lizzie.

Graham wheeled the laden trolley for them passed the check-out counter and then out to the car.

“Good luck with your new pet,” he said, “If you take good care of her, you’ll have a friend for life!”

“Thank you, I will,” replied Bev. She was almost bubbling over with excitement.

Back home Pat and Alice helped to carry everything upstairs, except for the carrier, which they left in the car for later. They soon had everything set up in the small spare room.

“This is perfect,” said Alice, “and don’t forget Bev, we’ll all help you.”

"Thanks" said Bev with a grateful smile as they followed Mrs. Cornhill, who had an old towel in her hand, out to the car again.

"See you later!" Pat shouted, as they drove away.

This time it was Tom himself who was waiting for them on the front steps as they arrived.

"Let's go this way to the barn." He said, as he reached into the car for the carrier.

"Here's the towel, Tom," said Mrs. Cornhill. "Will you wipe it over Molly for us?"

"I will, of course – give her a good rub down. She'll enjoy that, and then I'll do the other kittens as well. I always feel a little sorry for the mother cat as she has to say goodbye to her babies, but I think Molly will be very happy to be back inside the house. It's been a long time for her. We've given her lots of treats, and this time we are keeping one of the kittens for ourselves. She's been a good mother and she's trained the kittens well. They can all use the litter box, and they are fully weaned now. They've watched her eat and they can lap and eat fairly well. The vet was very happy with them."

"Thank you so much, Tom." Mrs. Cornhill said, looking at Tom gratefully.

"My pleasure," he replied, grinning at them all, as he opened the barn door.

Shortly after that, Bev was holding her kitten, as

Tom got busy with the towel, which he then placed in the carrier.

"Thank you so much for my kitten, Molly," said Bev as they turned to leave. The kitten had snuggled down on the towel and Tom took the carrier out to the car for them.

"Have you decided on a name yet, Bev?" he asked.

"I'm still deciding," replied Bev.

Bianca Parker came out to join them at the car. She handed Jill Cornhill a container of freshly baked cookies and a large bag of blueberry muffins.

"You know how I love to bake, and I always manage to make too much when the boys are away. When they are here, there never seems to be enough!" She laughed. "I know you have a full house at the moment, Jill."

"Thank you, yes, we have. This is very welcome, isn't it girls?" Jill Cornhill replied.

"Enjoy your kitten, Bev, and do let us know when you've named her, won't you?"

"I will, Bianca! Thank you." Bev called through the car window, as they waved goodbye.

"I'm taking Lizzie to visit her grandmother this afternoon, Bev, but I think this time you ought to stay at home and get to know your kitten. She'll be feeling strange and unsettled for a while, even with that towel. Everything will be new to her." Her mother said, as she turned into their driveway.

"I think so too. You don't mind, do you Liz? You'll be meeting your aunty from Portugal as well, won't you?"

"Yes," replied Lizzie, "Of course you must stay with your kitten, and I don't mind at all. I'm just grateful that you can take me, Mrs. Cornhill."

"It's a pleasure, dear."

"I've been thinking," said Lizzie. "What about calling your kitten 'Bluebell' Bev, because she has such lovely blue eyes."

"Oh, I like that! What do you think, Mom?"

"It sounds lovely! I do like that idea, Lizzie. How did you think of it?" asked Mrs. Cornhill.

"It's the name of my dorm, and I love it!

"Of course it is!" laughed Mrs. Cornhill.

"Bluebell she is then!" said Bev and she gave her friend a hug.

CHAPTER 26

Meeting Aunt Claudia

After another one of Jill Cornhill's excellent lunches, Lizzie washed her hands and face, brushed her hair very well and put on her best dress. She was so excited to be seeing her aunt, whom she had not seen for two years.

I've grown up a bit since then, she thought, at least I think I have, because so much has happened.

When she went downstairs, she found Mrs. Cornhill waiting for her at the front door.

"You look very nice, Lizzie," she said, smiling approvingly at her. "You must be very excited."

"Yes, I am. The last time I saw Aunt Claudia I think I was only seven. She has been to visit Granny more often, but just for short stays, before she and Uncle Mike leave on another one of their travels."

"Well then, she is in for a big surprise! You've

probably grown up a lot since then."

There was very little traffic on the roads, being a Sunday afternoon, and they were soon at the convalescent home.

Jill Cornhill and Lizzie found Mrs. Sinclair and Aunt Claudia already seated on the verandah.

"What a wonderful surprise this is, Lizzie, and how you have grown!" said her aunt coming forward to give her a big hug. "And you must be Mrs. Cornhill. I have just been hearing how kind you have been to our little girl, and Lizzie, I've heard how brave you have been through all your ordeals. My goodness, it's an absolute miracle the way you found your school! Do come and sit down, I want to hear it all over again!"

Lizzie hugged her grandmother and sat down in a chair beside her.

"Granny," she asked, "Have you heard anything more about my dad? I'm still worried about him?"

Her grandmother shook her head. "I'm afraid not, Lizzie. But don't worry. At least your mother is there to keep an eye on things. I do hope she is able to do that. A military field hospital might be out of bounds to visitors, what do you think, Claudia?"

Lizzie looked anxiously at her tall slim aunt, who was also very tanned from her recent time in Africa. How pretty she is, she thought, with her blond hair and bright blue eyes.

“You look quite a lot like Daddy, Aunt Claudia, I hadn’t remembered that. Were you good friends when you were growing up?”

“We were always the very best of friends, Lizzie,” she replied, “That is why I am so upset at the thought of all he has been through. It is all just too awful to imagine, but we must be positive, mustn’t we? I like to believe that they will both be home very soon. I’m just here for a short visit this time, but I’ll be here for much longer, once you go home, Mom. I’ll help you settle back into your own home again and perhaps John and Andrea will be home by then, too.”

“Oh, I do hope so,” cried Lizzie, squeezing her eyes shut, “but then what will happen to me? I love it at Oakwood and I even love being a boarder. I hope I’ll be allowed to stay.”

“I’m sure you will,” said her grandmother. “Miss Gorley is very pleased with the way you have settled down, despite everything, and your schoolwork is excellent. It would be a shame to move you again, wouldn’t it, Mrs. Cornhill?’

“Oh, please call me Jill, and yes, it would be a pity. My daughter Bev would be most upset, too, you have become such good friends, Lizzie.” Added Jill Cornhill.

A nurse brought out a tray of tea and cake and Claudia rose to pour it, while Lizzie handed round the cake.

"What a lovely place this is, Mom," said Claudia, waving a hand in the direction of the gardens.

"Wait till you see my school!" Lizzie exclaimed, "It's even more beautiful, isn't it, Mrs. Cornhill?" They all looked at Lizzie's smiling face.

"It certainly is Lizzie. I love it too, remember. It's my old school. I spent all my school years there!" she added, "right the way through from the age of five!"

CHAPTER 27

Back to School

"For our last meal before Lizzie has to go back, can we have a barbeque, Dad?" asked Bev. "Everyone will be home by then and it will be great fun."

"That's a great idea, Bev," her father replied, "Peter and Brian will enjoy that too." And so it was arranged.

Brian had returned from his holiday with his friend and was so full of tales of their various adventures, that it had been hard to slow him down for long enough to tell him about the kitten in the small spare room. Once he had eventually taken in what Bev was saying, he raced upstairs to meet Bluebell for the first time. Bev let him hold her kitten for a few minutes and she could tell that he loved her almost as much as she did.

"I'll help you look after her, if you like Bev. I get home from school earlier than you do sometimes. I'll take care of her then, okay?"

"That's kind of you, Brian, thanks." Bev said warmly.

Peter had a four-day break from his university and was very happy to spend the time at home. Susan asked if her boyfriend could join them for the barbeque. They would both be studying hard for their final exams during the coming weeks, and they would not be seeing each other for a while. Alice had gone home to her family for the last week of the holidays.

At almost the last minute, Jill Cornhill invited the whole Parker family to join them, so the barbeque became a jolly party. Lizzie enjoyed herself so much, she didn't want the day to end. With her suitcase packed, except for her night things and her uniform, she climbed into bed, thinking that this had been the most wonderful holiday she had ever had. She had said goodbye to her Aunt Claudia on her last visit to her grandmother. She promised to write to both of them very soon. She hoped that she would have news of her parents. Since the fax to her grandmother, they had heard nothing more. Lizzie hoped, as she fell asleep, that there would be a letter waiting for her at school.

In the late afternoon, Mrs. Cornhill drove Lizzie back to Oakwood and wished her a happy term.

"Perhaps you can come to us at half-term Lizzie," she said, as she hugged her goodbye.

"I'd really love that, and thank you for having me, Mrs. Cornhill. I will miss you all and Bluebell, too. I've had a wonderful time."

Lizzie made her way down to the dorm buildings and then up to Bluebell dorm.

Mary was already there, and they chatted as they unpacked. Then Lizzie went to find Matron Jordan, to find out if there was a letter for her, but sadly, there wasn't.

"I will just have to be patient then, I suppose," she told Matron, with tears in her eyes.

"Yes, you will, dear, I'm afraid, but do try not to worry. You know what they say – no news is good news! Perhaps it will be this time too."

"I hope you're right," said Lizzie, and she tried hard not to cry, as she made her way back to the dorm.

Supper that night was a noisy affair with everyone excitedly telling friends about their holiday adventures. Lizzie told about the new kitten and their visits to the ice rink. She did not mention any of her family, not even Aunt Claudia's visit. What was the point? She was glad when the meal was finally over, even though it had been a special one, as it always was on their first night back at school. Lizzie wondered briefly if Matron would come and read to them. She hoped it would be the next book in the Harry Potter series. She had so enjoyed the first one. If not, she thought, I'll just have to borrow it from the library.

By the time it was "lights out", Lizzie found that she was very tired indeed, as she tucked her teddy in beside her. She fell asleep with the comforting thought that tomorrow might just bring her that long awaited letter from her mother.

CHAPTER 28

Another surprise phone call

It was Wednesday evening in the middle of their third week of term. Lizzie had not yet received a single letter from her mother, and she was getting pretty desperate. What was it that Matron had said? Oh, yes, that no news was good news, or something like that. At that moment, Lizzie didn't think it was. That's just a silly saying, she thought. How could no news be a good thing? She closed her eyes as tightly as she could and hoped with all her might that there would be a letter for her tomorrow. There MUST be, she told herself. I've waited long enough, Mom.

The girls were making their way upstairs after supper to get ready for bed and story time with Matron, when a senior girl rushed up to Lizzie.

"Are you Elizabeth Sinclair?" she asked.

"Yes." said Lizzie hesitantly.

"Come with me quickly, there's a phone call for you!" and grabbing Lizzie's arm she led her quickly in the direction of the senior dormitories, where juniors were usually not allowed to go.

"The call came through on our extension, Lizzie, don't worry, it's all right as long as you're with me. I'm Bexley Wilcox, by the way, and I'm a prefect."

"Oh, Bexley!" exclaimed Lizzie, "Of course I've heard all about you! You're our sports star and the main sports captain! I'm so pleased to meet you at last!" They arrived at the telephone in the entrance way to the senior dorms. Bexley picked up the receiver. "I've got Elizabeth here for you. Thank you for holding on." She handed the phone to Lizzie.

"Hello?" said Lizzie, a little hesitantly.

"Hello dear!" said her grandmother. "I asked the nurse to get the number for me and she must have made a mistake. I was too excited to put through the call myself. I've had another fax from your mother! A longer one this time. She wrote that the military hospital is releasing John, so that he can be flown home to see a doctor here, just for a check-up. The other three soldiers are also being released. They will all be flown home as soon as possible. Your mother has been given special permission to fly home with them. So they ought to be back in your hometown by the weekend. Your mother wrote that as soon as your dad is able to, they will come down here, Lizzie, and I'm to go home too! My physiotherapist is quite satisfied with my progress, and so is the occupational therapist, who said that as long as I will not be alone, she is quite satisfied. Your mom and dad will stay with me for a while."

"Oh, Gran! That's wonderful! I'm so happy! Matron said when I hadn't heard from Mom for so long, that no news is good news, and she was right. It couldn't be better."

"Yes," said her grandmother. "It couldn't be better. Now you had better go back to your own dorm and get a good night's rest, and so will I! Goodnight, dear and lots of love." And with that, her grandmother ended the call.

Bexley, who had waited patiently during the call, walked Lizzie back to the Junior dorm, where she quickly got ready for bed.

"I've had some very good news at long last, Mary" she said to her friend in the next bed. "I'll tell you about it in the morning!"

The next morning after assembly, Lizzie made her way to Miss Gorley's office to tell her the good news, too.

"Now isn't that wonderful! Just what you have

been waiting to hear. Now you can relax and just enjoy all your lessons."

"I'm still a bit worried, Miss Gorley," Lizzie replied, "you see, I love Oakwood and I love being a boarder and I don't want to leave."

"I hope you won't have to Lizzie. You have settled down here so well, even with all your troubles and you've made some good friends. Let's see what happens. Go to your classroom now and tell Miss Price your good news! She'll be very pleased for you too."

Lizzie joined her class as quickly as she could. Not wanting to disturb the lesson, she waited until the bell rang and then she put up her hand.

"Yes, Lizzie?" asked Miss Price.

"I've got some news I'd like to share with everyone, Miss Price. Would that be okay?"

"Go ahead, dear," said Miss Price with a smile.

Lizzie made her way to the front and faced everyone.

"You may or may not know that my father is a soldier and that he was reported missing in action, with three other soldiers. They were found eventually, and they all had to go into hospital for treatment. Well, I've just been told that they are on their way home at last. My mother, who is a journalist and who was with them in the war zone, is travelling back with them. I just wanted you all to know, because I know I have often been too sad to be a really good friend. Only Bev and Miss Price knew about my dad before. That's all I wanted to say Miss Price, thank you," said Lizzie turning to her teacher.

"That certainly is very good news, Lizzie." Miss Price replied, and the whole class clapped, as Lizzie made her way back to her seat. Her best friend Beverley jumped up and hugged her.

"I'm so happy for you!" she exclaimed.

CHAPTER 29

Several days later

Lizzie received another phone call, this time to Matron's office. Matron was smiling as she handed her the receiver.

"Hello, this is Lizzie."

"Hello, darling! This is your mom!" said a familiar and very dear voice. "We're home at last!"

"Oh, Mom, mom I'm so happy! Lizzie almost shouted into the phone, and she began to cry.

"Daddy has just seen our family doctor and a specialist and when he's more rested, we'll fly down and stay with granny for a while."

"That's the best news ever!" sniffed Lizzie, wiping away her tears.

"We'll have a good long chat when I see you, Lizzie, it won't be too long now and I'm simply longing to hear all about your new school and I want to meet your new friends, too. I can't believe how brave you have been, darling. I've just been talking about that with your Matron. Thank you for being so sensible and for not making a fuss. I know how hard this has been for you. I'll say goodnight now and we'll see each other very soon."

"Goodnight, Mom and please give my love to Daddy and hug him for me. Big hugs to you, too!"

Lizzie was beaming as she ran back to Bluebell dorm. It is all going to be okay, she thought, and when they see Oakwood, they will want me to stay. I know they will.

CHAPTER 30

How it all ended

Lizzie's parents arrived just in time for half term. There was a very happy reunion and when Mrs. Cornhill heard the news, she invited them all to lunch on the Sunday. All the Parkers were there too, as they considered John Sinclair a hero and wanted to hear firsthand, all that had happened to him and to the other three soldiers.

The weather had turned chilly, so they had the meal inside and somehow managed to fit around the very big table in the Cornhill's dining room. It was a great meal and a festive party with much talk and laughter. Bianca Parker invited them all out to the farm the next day, for a real farmhouse tea, after which the men went to look around the farm. John Sinclair was most impressed.

Everyone agreed that Lizzie had been a very

brave girl, with all she had faced, often all on her own. Her grandmother was particularly proud of her and said so several times.

Lizzie took her parents and grandmother to meet Miss Gorley, once the long weekend was over. They also went on a tour of the school.

"Isn't this just the very best school in the world?" said Lizzie, as they looked around Bluebell dorm.

"It is certainly most impressive," replied her father.

"It's lovely, darling," added her mother. "We are so glad that you are happy here and you'll be even happier to know that dad and I have decided to let you stay. You've made such good friends and your schoolwork, by all accounts, has been very good. You deserve to stay, darling. Dad and I have a lot to think about and to decide about our own future. He might even retire from the army now, and if that happens, who knows? We might just find ourselves down here, too. How would you like that?"

In answer, Lizzie hugged them both in turn.

Things couldn't be much better, could they? She thought, as she waved her parents and grandmother goodbye at the gate.

Some wishes do come true in the end, don't they? And with that, a much happier Elizabeth Sinclair ran off to find her friends.

ABOUT THE AUTHOR

R.A. Kahn was born in Cape Town, South Africa. She has had a long and varied career in education; the retail book trade; fund raising for a children's charity; events planning and as an author. Her hobbies are reading, writing, arts and crafts, and gardening. After living in several countries in Africa, she has now retired to Jerusalem, Israel.